PENGUIN BOOKS
THE BIRTH AND DEATH
OF THE MIRACLE MAN

ALBERT WENDT was born in Western Samoa in 1939.
In 1952 he was awarded a government scholarship to
study in New Zealand. He attended New Plymouth
Boys' High School, Ardmore Teachers' College, and
the Victoria University of Wellington, where he
gained an M.A. in history. In 1965 he returned to
Western Samoa to teach, and soon afterwards became
Principal of Samoa College. In 1974 he took up an
appointment at the University of the South Pacific,
and later moved to the University of the South Pacific
Centre in Western Samoa, where he became Director.
His other novels include *Sons for the Return Home*, *Pou-
liuli*, and *Leaves of the Banyan Tree* (Penguin), and he
has written a collection of short stories, *Flying-Fox in a
Freedom Tree* and a volume of poetry, *Inside us the Dead*.

# The Birth and Death of the Miracle Man

*A Collection of Short Stories*

ALBERT WENDT

PENGUIN BOOKS

Penguin Books Ltd, Harmondsworth, Middlesex, England
Viking Penguin Inc., 40 West 23rd Street, New York, New York 10010, U.S.A.
Penguin Books Australia Ltd, Ringwood, Victoria, Australia
Penguin Books Canada Limited, 2801 John Street, Markham, Ontario, Canada L3R 1B4
Penguin Books (N.Z.) Ltd, 182–190 Wairau Road, Auckland 10, New Zealand

First published by Viking 1986
Published in Penguin Books 1987

Reproduced, printed and bound in Great Britain by
Hazell Watson & Viney Limited,
Member of the BPCC Group,
Aylesbury, Bucks

*For Konai and Randy*

# Contents

# Acknowledgements

'A Talent' – published in *Landfall*, New Zealand.

'The Birth and Death of the Miracle Man' – published in *Hemisphere*, Australia.

'Elena's Son' – published in *MANA*, Fiji.

'Exam Failure Praying' – published in *Education*, New Zealand.

'The Balloonfish and the Armadillo' – published in *Australian Bulletin*.

'Prospecting' – published in *Échos du Commonwealth*.

'I Will be Our Saviour from the Bad Smell' – published in *Islands*, New Zealand.

'Birthdays' – published in *Landfall*, New Zealand.

'Daughter of the Mango Season' – published in *Landfall*, New Zealand.

# GLOSSARY

| | |
|---|---|
| aiga | family, extended family |
| aitu | ghost, spirit |
| alia | double-hulled canoe |
| ali'i | matai who holds an ali'i title |
| alofa | love, compassion |
| alu | go, to go |
| atua | god |
| fa'a Samoa | Samoan way of doing things, Samoan way of life |
| fale | Samoan house |
| fau | species of hibiscus |
| fautasi | long boat rowed by oarsmen |
| fono | council |
| ifi | chestnut |
| lape | game, like rounders |
| lavalava | skirt-like wrap-around garment |
| lotu | church service, act of worship |
| ma'i aitu | illness attributed to/caused by an aitu |
| malae | meeting area |
| mana | (supernatural) power |
| matai | titled head of an aiga |
| oso | planting stick |
| paepae | raised stone foundation of a fale |
| papalagi ⎫ palagi ⎭ | person of European stock |
| pua | gardenia |
| pulu | coastal tree |
| sau'ai | ogre |
| sauali'i | respectful term for aitu |
| taro | root crop |
| taula aitu | priest of an aitu |
| taulasea | traditional healer |
| tiputa | woman's upper garment |
| to'ona'i | Sunday lunch |
| tufuga | craftsman, e.g. carpenter, tattooist |
| tu'ua | senior orator in a village |
| umu | stone oven |

# A Talent

It hadn't rained for over a month and, sitting in his fale, which was the smallest one in Sapepe village, Salepa (everyone called him Sale) cursed the endless heat and the flies and the stench of the mangroves and the shrieking of his neighbour's children and the audibly complaining hunger in his belly and his wife Lagilelei (everyone called her Lagi), who had left him, taking their three children with her, the week before. After cursing his wife – calling her a mean, sullen, ungrateful, ugly bitch who had sucked the marrow out of his gullible bones for eighteen years – he re-cursed all the other things he had cursed before cursing his wife. The fourth time he did this, he was a pulsating bundle of angry muscle and mouth and breath cursing the whole 'sinful planet' (his phrase) and the whole meaningless forty-four years of suffering (for no reason at all) which had brought him to that September without rain and the moaning of his empty belly.

His mother, Fa'aluma, who he thought was out in the kitchen fale cooking him a meal, entered the fale quietly, and he didn't notice her until she pulled out her basket from under their only bed and then turned to leave again. 'Where are you going?' he asked her. (Now in her sixty-seventh year, she was bent and shrivelled like a crooked orator's staff onto which a meagre distribution of flesh had been fastened; she reminded him of an

11

underfed sow which had given birth to a gluttonous brood of piglets.) She continued to leave, and he remembered she was deaf in one ear (the left one). 'Where are you going?' he almost shouted.

Without turning or stopping, she said, 'Out!'

'To where?' he called. No reply, only the sound of her feet shuffling out of his hearing. So he cursed her too, called her a sour and ignorant woman whom he didn't deserve as a mother.

He got a pillow, which was stained with coconut oil, off the bed, flung it down on to the floor, thumped his head back into it as he lay down and tried to sleep. Found he couldn't, not with the heat and the flies and the mangrove stench and his hunger and his wife and children and now his mother deserting him.

After what seemed an hour, his body blistered with sweat, he realized with even more depressing depression, as it were, that no other family in Sapepe had ever deserted their matai – it just wasn't done. Everyone was going to accuse him of having been mean and heartless and cruel towards his family. (For a mother to leave her son was irrevocable proof that her son was a stone-hearted ingrate.) Trust everyone to blame him and not his ungrateful family! But did he have any choice – no one was going to believe him. He had to get his family back, and stop his village from ridiculing him for a sin he wasn't guilty of. Anyway, he asked himself, who were going to serve him as a matai? Who were to cultivate the plantation, cook his food, and do all those chores meant only for women and untitled males? His belly roared more hungrily and convinced him further to get his wife back (and she wasn't really a bad woman, at least she didn't nag him and she was a good cook and she did satisfy his modest sexual needs – and the more he thought about this, and his modest sexual needs became more immodest, so to speak politely, the more he was persuaded he wanted her back); he also needed his mother and children – they respected him (and he admitted to himself that there weren't many people who respected him), and he did love them, for wasn't it a sin for a father not to love, treasure, cherish and console his own flesh and blood?

But how was he going to get them back? This question hit him in the core of his head like an expertly delivered right hook, and forced him up to a sitting position, his left hand clutching at his forehead. He couldn't just go to her and, in front of her whole pretentious family (who were nobodies), *plead* with her to return with the children – it wasn't proper or fitting for a matai (and a man) to humiliate himself that way. No. No, he wasn't going to ask them back! But as his hunger squirmed more painfully, he tried to force himself to swallow his pride: he would only have to humiliate himself once, other men wouldn't hold it against him, and he could always make it appear that she was deliberately humiliating him (and in public at that). Later, he concluded it wasn't proper him considering this important problem while he was desperately hungry, a hungry person wasn't logical, he'd think about it after he had eaten. Remembered that his mother, who was supposed to have prepared his meal, had gone, and he nearly wept with frustrated, hungry anger.

He got up reluctantly (it was absolutely beneath the dignity of a matai to cook his own food), went into the kitchen fale (and it was difficult for his empty stomach to carry his huge body there), started a fire, and put some bananas (there was nothing else to eat) on it to boil. While the bananas boiled, he searched the fale for some money to buy some tinned fish or meat to go with the bananas. Flung everything aside. No money. She had taken it all. Tried not to weep. Decided to go to the only store in Sapepe and get some food on credit. Remembered they already owed a lot of money, and Tauilopepe, the owner of the store, had told them they weren't allowed any more credit. Arse! Arse! Arse! he swore aloud.

Through the falling darkness and the thick crying of the cicadas he hurried to the store, avoiding being seen by anyone; waited under the breadfruit trees outside the store until all the other customers had left, and then entered and found only Tauilopepe sitting behind the counter, reading a magazine.

As always, the store smelled of kerosene. Salepa didn't hesitate: tears started streaming down his face as he moved up to the counter and gazed at Tauilopepe who looked up, saw the tears, and asked, with obvious concern, 'What has happened, Sale?'

'My wife and children,' he replied. 'My poor wife and children!' More tears.

Tauilopepe was the wealthiest and most powerful matai in Sapepe, but, as Salepa had discovered years before, under the hard exterior of the shrewd business-man, was the soft heart of the failed theological student Tauilopepe had been in his youth; or, in other words, an easy touch if one knew the correct way to touch. 'Has some trouble happened to your family?' Tauilopepe asked.

Salepa swallowed and wiped his tears with a corner of his tattered lavalava. 'As you know, sir, they – my poor family, that is – went to visit her family last week: her old mother is very ill – dying, they tell me.' Paused. More tears.

'Yes?' Tauilopepe prompted him.

'I need to go to them,' replied Salepa. 'One of my children – you know, my little son Amiga – is very, very ill, sir.' Wiped his tears again, noticed that he had convinced Tauilopepe, and said, 'I need your help, sir. This poor worthless person needs your help, sir!'

'Will $5 do?' asked Tauilopepe.

Salepa nodded his head. 'Thank you, sir. I also need some food to take to them. As you well know, sir, my wife's family is very poor!'

Salepa left the store a few minutes later with three tins of herrings in tomato sauce (his favourite), three tins of corned beef (again his favourite brand), $5 clutched in his left hand, and two large tins of powdered milk for his 'sick son'.

That night he ate a tin of herrings and a tin of corned beef with the bananas. Then, feeling dizzy from over-eating, his large belly now weighing him down, he showered in his neighbour's shower as was his family's practice because his family didn't have a shower of their own. (His neighbour, Sava, was a distant cousin so he *was* family.)

He decided to visit Apia the next day, see a cowboy picture maybe, and then, on his way home, call in and see his wife, children and mother. No need to hurry.

He fell asleep thinking of his son: he was sure the boy would blossom into an important and wealthy man, like Tauilopepe, who would care for him in his old age.

He was up early the next morning because he wanted to catch the first bus into Apia where he would breakfast at the Savalalo Market on hot pancakes and tea – a luxury he didn't enjoy often enough. Before showering, he realized he needed a shave so he borrowed his neighbour's razor; as usual, he promised to replace the blade. He put on his one and only good shirt (a white one which he wore to church every Sunday), and his only unpatched lavalava (a black one which he had borrowed the year before from his brother who lived and worked in Apia as a government driver), and his only belt (a thick leather one which he had stolen the previous Xmas from one of the town stores). He whistled as he combed his hair, realized he needed some hair oil, thought of his cousin Sava but persuaded himself not to, as there was a limit to the generosity of any human being, even a blood relative, and decided he would buy a tin of brilliantine (his favourite brand) in Apia that day – thanks to Tauilopepe's generosity.

When the bus stopped in front of him, he noticed it was full, so he injected an expression of pain into his face and then limped up to and into the bus. Most of the passengers in the front seats noticed his limp, and three of them stood up and asked him to sit down. Thanking them, he sighed as he sagged into the nearest seat just behind the driver. The young man, who had given him the seat and who was now standing in the aisle, offered him a cigarette but he refused it, saying he was very ill and was on his way to Apia Hospital to consult a papalagi doctor there.

After consuming twelve pancakes and four mugs of hot tea, he wandered round the market, pretending he was going to buy some food: he'd examine the taro or bananas, ask after the price, the vendor would quote it, and he'd shake his head, mutter Too much! Too much!, and move on to the next vendor. One of the taro vendors, a Sapepean he knew well, asked him why he was all dressed up. Going to see the Public Works about a job, he replied. What kind of job? the man asked. Driving one of the Cabinet ministers' cars, he said; and, before the man could ask him where he had learned to drive, he said he had to hurry or he'd be late for his appointment. Only a few paces away, he gasped, stopped, fumbled in his shirt pocket, and then returned to the taro vendor.

'Think I've lost all my money!' he said. 'Or some Apia thief has stolen it!' Searched in his pocket again, this time more frantically. 'How am I going to go home?'

'Can I help?' the vendor asked.

'No, the money should be in my clothes somewhere,' he said, re-searching the folds of his lavalava and then his shirt pocket.

'Here, take this,' the vendor offered, stuffing a dollar note into Salepa's shirt pocket.

'No, no, no!' protested Salepa and tried to return the money but the man pushed his hand away.

Two Sapepe vendor victims later, Salepa had collected a further $4. He now had $9.25 altogether, and it was only mid-morning. He went to the fish counters, found he couldn't get up to the front because of the bustling crowd, again pretended he was crippled in his left leg, and one lady, who looked like the wife of a pastor, asked if she could buy the fish he wanted for him. He thanked her, handed her $8 and told her to buy as many strings of fish as possible – he needed the fish for his daughter's wedding that evening, he added. He watched her fight her way through the crowd.

She handed him the basket in which she had put the strings of fish she had bought for him. Eight strings at a dollar a string, she told him. He thanked her and started limping away from her, with the basket. She rushed up to him and shoved a dollar note into his shirt pocket. To help with his daughter's wedding, she whispered to him.

He sold seven strings to various people at $1.50 each, as he went along Beach Road; kept one string for his brother Folo, the driver at P.W.D. $12.75 he had now. And he whistled as he went to see his brother.

Folo, who had left Sapepe nearly ten years before, had eight children (five were attending school and the fees were high), lived in a rented fale (more a shack than a fale) on rented land (a half-filled-in swamp section at Fugalei), was perpetually consulting one traditional healer after another to try and cure his ever-aching stomach, and was earning only about $35 a month. Unlike other Sapepeans who envied their relatives who worked for wages in Apia, and especially those who were government employees, Salepa didn't envy his brother at all: Folo was too obedient, servile and unimaginative, and deserved all the suffering, especially the aching guts, he was receiving.

His brother gladly accepted the string of fish – unlike Salepa, he hadn't eaten that morning. He had been out fishing most of the night but hadn't caught much, Salepa said to him. Folo asked how their mother was. She was healthier than ever and sent him her blessings and she needed some money for her church donation that Sunday, Salepa replied. Again unlike Salepa, Folo never refused any requests from his mother, and Salepa knew this. He didn't have any money on him, said Folo, but he'd go and borrow some from his supervisor. How much was needed? Folo asked. Three dollars would be enough, replied Salepa.

Salepa couldn't control his curiosity, as though he wanted to savour every detail of Folo's suffering, when Folo returned and gave him the money. How much did he have to pay back to his supervisor? he asked Folo. $3 plus twenty per cent interest, Folo replied, his eyes gazing at his feet. A lot of money, remarked Salepa, folding up the $3 and sheathing it in his shirt pocket.

On his way back to the market for lunch, Salepa wondered why such a person as Folo – and he did love him – continued to tolerate such a humiliating fate.

After lunching on two large helpings of chop suey, rice and taro, which he paid 80 cents for, he counted his money under the table (there were innumerable thieves in Apia). $14.95. Excellent take, the best he had made so far in one morning, he congratulated himself.

Still two hours before the matinée started.

On his way along the waterfront towards the Tivoli Theatre, he came across a small poker game taking place under one of the pulu trees. He stopped and, with a scatter of onlookers, watched the three men who were playing. He knew that such games were illegal but he just couldn't resist it when one of the players threw in his cards and left. From their appearance, the two remaining players looked really formidable Apians, well-schooled in all the arts of relieving unwary villagers of their money.

'May I?' Salepa asked. One of the players, a stringy man with a badly pock-marked face and a thin moustache and a large bald spot and thick dirty hands, nodded to him to sit down.

'Where are you from?' asked his partner who, bare to the waist to reveal rippling muscles and an eagle tattoo on his chest, had a stye in his left eye.

18

'From a village in the back.' Salepa deliberately used a favourite expression employed by Apians to emphasize their pretension of superiority to villagers.

'Which village?' the stye-eyed one asked as he shuffled the cards. Salepa gave him the name of the remotest village on Upolu. He noticed (but deliberately ignored) the wink which Stye-Eyed gave his friend; he now knew what kind of poker the two Apians, Stye-Eyed and Dirty-Hands, wanted to play with him.

'Are we playing for money?' he asked.

Stye-Eyed and Dirty-Hands looked at each other in disbelief. 'Yes,' Stye-Eyed replied, 'but the stakes aren't high. We're only playing for fun.'

'Five cents?' Salepa asked, taking out all his money so they could see it and be overcome with greed.

Dirty-Hands nodded, his eyes caressing Salepa's money. 'Five cents down but you can bet up to ten cents. Is that all right?'

'As long as it's for fun,' said Salepa. He tossed five cents into the centre. His opponents did the same.

Stye-Eyed dealt out the cards after Salepa had cut the pack.

Salepa lost $2 quickly. He asked one of the onlookers for the time. One hour before the matinée. 'Got to go soon,' he informed the others. 'How about raising the stakes to ten cents and up to twenty cents betting?' Stye-Eyed and Dirty-Hands agreed greedily. And Salepa lost another $2 in one game. He suggested doubling the stakes as he could only play three more hands because he had to be at the police station at 2 p.m.

'Why are you seeing the police?' Dirty-Hands asked.

'The Commissioner is my relative. Have to see him about some family business.'

Both Stye-Eyed and Dirty-Hands couldn't believe it when Salepa won the next three hands and $8 of their money, got up and said he really had to go.

'But you can't just leave with all our money!' Stye-

Eyed protested, his milky-white eye gazing threateningly at Salepa.

'You've got to give us a chance to win our money back!' threatened Dirty-Hands.

'Who says?' Salepa asked. 'As I've told you already, I've got to see my cousin, the Commissioner of Police.'

'He's not your cousin!' challenged Dirty-Hands.

'Want to find out?' asked Salepa. 'Just touch any part of me and you'll find out soon enough!'

As he moved away, he heard Stye-Eyed calling, 'Some day, fat man, we'll fix you!' Salepa turned and waved to them with the hand in which he was holding the money he had won off them.

He now had over $20.

Too full from lunch and disappointed with the western because there wasn't much fighting in it (and he didn't understand a word of all that English), he had fallen asleep half-way through the film. People near him had to wake him up repeatedly so as to try and rid their ears of his loud snoring. Now, as he waited in front of the market for his bus, he found he was hungry again, so he bought two pineapple pies and a large bottle of orange soft drink, devoured them, and then bought six loaves of fresh bread, two dozen coconut buns, some butter, and a tin of jam to take to his wife and her nobody family.

The bus swerved and they were round the last bend and into his wife's village. Surreptitiously so the other passengers wouldn't notice, he folded the paper money round the loose change, leaving out only $2, and carefully hid the money under the back of his belt. His wife's family was located in the middle of the village beside the church. He called to the driver to stop, and got off the bus, with his arms wrapped tightly around his large parcel of food.

He refused to lower his head as he walked towards the main fale of his wife's family, sensing they were all watching him and castigating him and joking about his size and just behaving rudely like the nobodies that they were. He couldn't see his wife or mother or children anywhere. Arse to them all! he swore under his breath.

Once inside the fale and seated cross-legged on the floor and leaning back against the centre front post, Salepa was greeted in the customary way by his wife's father, Sosoatu, a lean fisherman who possessed a lackadaisical silence about him similar to the sea's silence at night. Sosoatu's oratory was slow but enthusiastic and mentioned nothing about what was wrong between them. Salepa's reply, as usual, was exaggerated, over-enthusiastic, and similarly avoided any mention of what was wrong between them. While Salepa orated, he looked around the fale and then into the kitchen fale and then into the nearby fale that belonged to the family, but he couldn't see his wife or children or mother anywhere. After the formal greetings, the two men talked, with Salepa, as usual, doing most of the talking as he couldn't tolerate any lengthy pauses in any conversation he was involved in. An hour or so later, evening settling down over the village, Salepa still couldn't see his family anywhere but he wasn't going to ask.

Before the hurricane lamp was lit, all of Sosoatu's family – his wife and ten children and their children and a numerous assortment of other relatives – came into the fale. As was the practice, it was time for evening lotu. (All through it, everyone would avoid looking at Salepa, as if he was invisible.) After the hymn and Bible reading, Sosoatu acknowledged that Salepa wasn't invisible by asking him to say the prayer. The theme of Salepa's prayer was forgiveness: he pleaded with God to teach each and everyone of them to forgive one another; he emphasized the importance of forgiveness between husband and wife. When he opened his eyes at the end of his prayer, he saw his wife and children sitting among the people at the back posts of the fale.

They immediately left with everyone for the kitchen fale to prepare the evening meal.

At meal-time, as was the custom, the elders, Sosoatu and Salepa, were to eat first and be served by everyone else. Ponaivi, Salepa's eldest daughter who was eighteen years old but still without noticeable breasts, brought him his food on a food-mat. He smiled at her. Her face, which she turned away immediately, remained an unforgiving blank.

He took his anger out on his food, eating every morsel.

After the meal, during which his wife's mother (a fat woman with a permanent scowl on her face) had refused to speak to him, Fusi, his second and most favourite daughter (he was proud of her beauty which was already turning the heads of every male in Sapepe), brought him a towel, a clean lavalava, and some soap. He thought she would smile at him; she didn't.

He returned from his shower to find himself alone in the spaciously large fale (even Sosoatu was nowhere in sight). A mosquito net, obviously meant for him, had been strung up at one end of the fale. Arse to them all! he swore under his breath as he whistled and combed his hair and sat down in front of the net as if he wasn't concerned about anything. Arse to all them nobodies, including his daughters who were acting exactly like their nobody relatives!

A short while later, Sosoatu entered and told him that he was sorry he couldn't stay and keep him company as he had to attend a church meeting at the pastor's house, and left quickly. So there he was – all alone in an empty fale, with the hurricane lamp hanging from the rafters, ablaze with accusing light for all the inhabitants of his wife's nobody village to see he was all alone and being punished for having been cruel to his own flesh and blood.

He lay down on the pillow and the sleeping-mats in the net and pretended he was asleep, forgetting it was very, very early. She'd come to him in the night and beg for his forgiveness, he thought.

She didn't.

This game continued for three days and three nights during which time Salepa optimistically expected Lagi, his wife, to visit him at night, but she never did; he also expected his children, especially his ten-year-old son Amiga, to at least smile at him, but they didn't. (His family didn't even sleep in the same fale as him.) He was treated as an important but unwelcome guest: he was confined to the main fale from the time he awoke in the mornings to the time he went to sleep at night, provided with food, clothes and conversation with Sosoatu during meal-times, but, like a guest, he wasn't invited to participate in any family activities. When he offered to go fishing with Sosoatu, who usually went fishing every day except Sunday, Sosoatu told him he wasn't going that day. Early one morning he saw his daughter Ponaivi cutting the grass outside the kitchen fale, and he went out to help her but, as soon as she saw him, she ambled off to the tap where her mother was washing a large pile of clothes. During meal-times, when his wife and children helped serve him his food, he tried to look for a chance to speak to any one of them but no opportunity was ever allowed him by his watchful opponents. So during the daytime, he played patience with a pack of cards which he found on top of the family food-safe, and tried to devise a way of defeating them; he also made numerous trips to the family lavatory which was situated on stilts about twenty yards from the shore over a rickety causeway made of stones and hunks of coral; and he didn't care that he was doing all this in full view of his wife's family and village. Arse to them all; he'd wait them out; they'd soon tire of feeding him, having him around as an expensive guest, and they'd either hint to him that he leave, or come out openly and discuss the trouble between them.

Nothing of the sort happened for a few more days; and it wasn't until Sunday after to'ona'i that he found the opportunity to talk to Lagi. He didn't go with Sosoatu to the pastor's house for to'ona'i, not because he didn't want to, but because Sosoatu didn't invite him to; he ate alone in the main fale, served by many of Sosoatu's family, who, throughout the meal, once again avoided looking directly at him, but their ominously arrogant presence made him feel like an insect that was being scrutinized minutely and then being rejected as being worthless. He gobbled down his food and thanked them, no one said anything, they all got up and left to have their to'ona'i in one of the smaller family fale at the back, and left him gazing out at the lagoon flashing in the late morning light like a knife blade. Just as he was drifting off to sleep, he caught sight of Lagi taking a mat and pillow towards one of the shady mango trees near the rock fence bordering the family compound. She spread out the mat in the shade and then lay down on it. He pretended he was asleep but he observed the rest of the family until they were all asleep, then, pretending he was going to the plantation, he clambered over the rock fence, and crept along behind the fence until he was under the mango tree and behind the fence opposite his sleeping wife. He rested for a few moments, trying to control his breath and anger – and he was pulsating with anger: it was humiliating what he was doing, what his wife was *forcing* him to do. Then, after peeping over the fence and surveying the family compound and noting that nobody was awake, he climbed over the fence (and he was careful not to dislodge any of the rocks), and lay down in the narrow gap between the fence and Lagi, so her family wouldn't see him.

Only her face was exposed, a white sleeping-sheet covered the rest of her, and she was snoring softly through her slightly parted mouth. For what seemed an insane moment – and he nearly gave into it – he wanted to strangle her, yes, his hands wrapping around her fat

24

throat, his fingers digging in and in, forcing her rebellious tongue to unclench and lengthen out of her disobedient mouth dripping saliva and froth, her eyes bulging like the eyes of dead fish, her limbs twitching. She stirred and turned over to her left side and faced him and he broke from the spell.

Why he was spending all this time and effort and trouble and humiliation over that ungratefully cruel woman, he'd never fathom. She was bloody ugly as well. Once she had been quite comely, but such comeliness had disappeared into fat. He could get any women he desired, he thought. But could he? He shut his eyes and tried to obliterate the sight of a short fat man being laughed at by a group of children and women. Slowly, hesitantly, he opened his eyes and reached out and touched her lightly on her arm.

Her eyes blinked open and she stared at him. For a moment, he couldn't believe she was awake.

'Don't touch me!' she said and then turned her back to him.

'You were awake all the time?' he asked.

'I've got nothing to say to you!'

'You were awake all the time, weren't you?' he repeated, convinced that she had been awake and had *planned* for him to come to her. She maintained her silence. He clutched her shoulder and tried to turn her round to face him, but she shrugged off his hand. 'I'm talking to you!' he threatened.

'But I'm not talking to you!' she replied.

'Why did you plan this meeting then?' he asked.

'I didn't!'

'You did!'

'I didn't!'

'You did!'

'Keep your voice down!' she said. It was all so ridiculous, he realized suddenly, so he said nothing as he breathed his anger up into the tangled branches of the mango tree.

'Why did you do it?' she asked finally.

'Do what?' He pretended not to know what she was referring to. (He had *acquired* – and he never used any other word for it – $10 from their Sapepe pastor. Lagi had found out about it, and when she had castigated him for it, calling him a thief, he had beaten her with his fists.)

'You know what!' she said.

He sighed. 'I don't know what,' he said, his anger gone.

'Why did you steal that money?' she said.

'I didn't steal it,' he replied.

Ignoring his answer, she said, 'You promised you'd never do it again but you went right ahead and did it, and you did it to our Man of God!'

'He gave me the money,' he insisted.

'But you told him one of your stories. You lied to him.'

'Our pastor is a generous man. He has more than enough money to feed his family, whereas people like us don't. He was only helping us. And I'm going to pay him back anyway!' He reached over and caressed her shoulder, and this time she let him.

'Why can't you be like other men?' she asked. 'Why can't you be like Folo who has a steady job and supports his family that way? Or cultivate a plantation, or do something honest and honourable like that?'

'I'm no good at any of those. You know that, you've seen me trying for the last five years. In all that time, I never once used my only talent. I tried, Lagi. I really tried, but I couldn't bear being a failure any longer; I couldn't bear watching you and our children being hungry and poor. We couldn't even afford school fees for our children. I *had* to use my one and only talent. I couldn't help it any longer. Some men are born like me: our only talent may be against the law, but it's the only talent we possess. And you know what Jesus said about not wasting your talents.' He realized she was crying softly into her pillow. He caressed her shoulders and back as he continued whispering that he couldn't help what he was because God had meant him to be that way. Eventually, she turned over and faced him. Before she could say anything, he promised he would never again use his only talent to acquire money, and other things like that, from other people. Tears brimmed out of his eyes. She smiled at him and told him that it was time they all went back home to Sapepe, and that she was sorry she had left him. In turn he vowed he would never beat her again, and that if he ever broke this promise, may God strike him dead. Did she believe him? he asked. She smiled and nodded her head.

Women were so gullible, he thought, as they walked back to the main fale to pack their things for their return home.

The following morning when they returned to their fale in Sapepe, the money, which he had obtained in Apia, dropped out of his lavalava as he undressed. He stooped down quickly. Too late. Lagi had seen it. She picked it up and returned it to him as if nothing unexpected had occurred, and, by reacting in this unexpected manner, she immediately made him suspicious, but he took the money and put it in the large family chest where they kept all their clothes and valuables.

For the whole of that day and the next one, she mentioned nothing about the money to him, and he surmised that perhaps, like any other sensible wife who needed money to keep her family alive, she had reconciled herself to his talent. On Thursday night as they lay in their mosquito net, she informed him, casually, that she had used $15 of the money to pay their debt at Tauilopepe's store.

'But . . . but . . . ,' he started to protest, remembered his promise to her, stopped and whispered, 'That's good, very good.'

'We'll give the rest of the money as a donation to our

pastor this Sunday,' she said. And what are we going to use for money next week? he wanted to ask her but didn't when she moved over and embraced him and, in a few minutes, was expertly satisfying his modest sexual needs. He fell asleep believing she was the best wife any man could have.

On Monday afternoon, their son returned from school with a note demanding immediate payment of his school fees or he wouldn't be allowed back into school. Lagi read the note, handed it to Sale, and then left for the kitchen fale as if the note had nothing whatsoever to do with her. After lotu that evening, his mother, who had returned home a few days before after living with cousins in the next village, informed him that she needed $5 for Women's Committee affairs and that Lagi too needed money for the same purpose. Late into the night, the problem of where he was going to get the money from held him between its teeth and shook him, and he again cursed his fate and a September without rain.

Before daybreak, he woke Lagi and told her that he was going into town to see if he could borrow the money from Folo. He knew that she knew that he was lying, but was surprised when she did nothing to stop him. As he got into the bus, Lagi and their children and his mother waved to him as though they were giving him unconditional permission to use his talent to its most rewarding potential. Without any reservations his family – bless them! – had finally accepted who he was totally; they had seen the light and would never regret it, he concluded. In relation to his family, he could now be completely himself, openly, honestly, without shame.

At first, he went to Apia only once a week. (And sometimes, if his take was large, only once a fortnight.) His weekly take was never below $5, enough at first for what they needed to buy from the store and contribute towards Sapepe and family affairs. As time passed, however, the more money he brought home, the more money his family expected the next time he went in; his wife and mother expected new clothes, so did his daughters; instead of eating tinned fish, they now ate tinned corned beef and other expensive food daily; and every time he visited Apia, they expected him to return with exotic food such as apples, saveloys, salted beef, cabin bread, coconut buns, and finally, after he brought home $30, they asked him to buy them a radio, then, later on, a large wall mirror and tallboy and, later on still, sandals for everyone in their family; Lagi even got him to buy himself a second-hand woollen charcoal suit to wear to church. Consequently, three months after he started, he discovered he had to take more precarious risks to satisfy their demands. It became more and more difficult to find victims – people were beginning to recognize him. After he narrowly escaped being caught one afternoon, he returned home and told Lagi that he needed to stay out of Apia for at least a month. She ignored his plea and informed him that she and Fa'aluma had planned to visit Apia with the Women's Committee that Saturday and needed $10 for fares and spending money. It was impossible for him to *work* (and his whole family now used this word to describe his Apia activities) in Apia that week, he told her; she refused to satisfy his modest sexual needs that night (and the next two nights). On Thursday night, after he promised he would visit Apia the next day and get the money they needed, she rewarded him with her expert talent. (And he had to admit that this *was* her most precious talent which, once she had allowed him the right to legally exercise his only talent, she had developed to complement his talent in skill and intensity and demand: she now couldn't do without his talent, and he couldn't do without hers; one talent fed off the other, an insatiable and compulsive craving.)

After *acquiring* $15 from a group of taro vendors, he was arrested as he boarded the Sapepe bus that afternoon.

A week later, he was tried – Lagi refused to attend his trial – and sentenced to six months in prison.

His mother visited him a month afterwards in jail and informed him that Lagi had run off with another man (and how was she, a sick old woman, going to support his children? she asked). The following Friday, Ponaivi, his eldest daughter, who, because she was breastless, had always worried him, eloped with a youth from the next village; and Fusi, his favourite daughter, went off (against her grandmother's wishes) to live with her mother's family in Savai'i. His son Amiga was expelled from school for not paying his fees.

Arse, arse, arse! he cursed his fate. It was all God's fault for having created him with his peculiar talent.

# Justice

The most sensational trial in our country's recent history lasted ten exciting days.

I attended it (and so did a multitude of other concerned people). I had a reserved seat in the second row – the sergeant in charge of the court is my first cousin.

The accused (and throughout the trial everyone, including his own lawyer, hardly referred to him by his name but as *the accused*) had murdered a papalagi nun; and he was only twenty years old. At the start of his trial he kept insisting that he had loved her, that he was guilty of murder, and they should hang him, but the Judge, who was well-known for his benevolence and kindness and profound sense of fair play, ruled to give him a thoroughly fair trial. An expensive psychiatrist was even flown in from New Zealand to examine the accused. The psychiatrist, a nervously rotund papalagi who, while giving his hour-long evidence, spoke too softly and was therefore constantly asked by the Judge to speak up, pronounced the accused insane – something about him being 'psychotic and schizophrenic' (you know, the usual unintelligible jargon used by these charlatans!). He also argued that the accused was in urgent need of expert psychiatric treatment, preferably in another country, as Western Samoa didn't have adequate medical facilities to treat such a serious case. We all thought the Judge would terminate the case at

31

this point, but he didn't (and many of us were glad because of this). Twenty-five witnesses were called by the prosecution and cross-examined in elaborate detail; fifteen witnesses were called by the defence.

From their lengthy but fascinating evidence, I gathered that the accused had followed the nun – referred to throughout the trial by everyone as *the victim* – from the Convent at Vaelele and into and around the town, on the morning of Saturday, 20 May. When asked by the defence whether the victim had known he was following her, the accused said, 'Yes, she knew because she was in love with me and I was in love with her!' (We were all shocked by such blasphemy but forgave him because he was obviously insane.) After she had disappeared into one of the large stores, he had gone into the neighbouring hardware and had bought a bread-knife – he hadn't enough money to buy any other type of knife.

He had stood on the footpath, facing the doorway of the store into which his victim had gone, the knife hidden under his left arm pressed against his side. His victim came out and walked directly towards him, he declared, his eyes brimming with tears, and she was smiling at him and was stretching out her arms to embrace him. That was all he remembered, he said. Two vendors who were selling handicrafts in front of the store described how they had seen the accused raise the knife and, as his poor victim backed away, had plunged the knife into her left breast, and had then fled down the street, leaving the cruel knife (referred to in the trial as Exhibit A) in his unfortunate and innocent victim. One of the vendors, an extremely large woman with eyes that bulged in excitement as she described, with frantic relish, her role in the drama, had rushed forward, caught the falling victim whose immaculately white habit was now stained with blood, and had cradled her anguished head in her lap. This witness maintained – and we all believed her – that the victim, while dying in her abundant arms, had smiled softly and had whispered that her slayer was to be forgiven. At this juncture in the trial, the accused jumped to his feet and shouted that he didn't deserve to be forgiven because he was guilty of murdering that beautiful, sacred lady, and had to be hanged for it! The Judge ignored his plea and continued with the trial.

One of the last people to take the witness stand was the father of the accused – a venerable old man who was reputed to be highly respected in his village for his wisdom, justice and generosity. He wept as he spoke, asking that his family be forgiven for his evil son's most evil crime. His son – and he found it difficult to call such an 'animal' his son – had run away from home three years before to live with his mother's family (his mother had died a few years previously) and had obviously got into bad company. The old man claimed that his son was *not* insane – none of his other seven sons or three daughters was – and concluded by pleading with the Court to hang the son who had disgraced him and his family and village before God and their beloved country. We were all moved (and many of the women were crying) by the old man's performance and felt completely sorry for him; he and his family would never be able to live down such a disgrace. (I vowed then and there that if any of my sons – and I have four of them, one is the same age as the accused – ever disgraced me that way, I would hang him myself, and it wouldn't matter one iota if he was insane!)

The Court sentenced the accused to life imprisonment after declaring him insane; he was also to get medical treatment overseas at the expense of the State. The father of the accused sprang up and, beating his face with his fists, pleaded once again – and quite correctly so – that his son be hanged and then buried in a nameless grave.

As two policemen started leading out the accused, he turned, bowed to the crowd, and declared that he had loved her and should therefore be hanged for killing her. Walking past his father, who was now weeping, the accused paused for a breathless moment and whispered something into his father's ear. His father recoiled in horror and, with a pitiful gasp, collapsed to the floor in a dead faint.

A month later, a day before he was to be taken to New Zealand for treatment, the accused hanged himself in his cell.

To this day I keep asking people who were at the trial if they know what the accused had whispered to his father. No one seems to know, and his father, who we hear is now decrepitly sick and never leaves his fale, has never told anyone.

Before writing this, I tried to remember the names of the accused and his victim but I found I couldn't (and still can't). I can also only remember one unusual feature about the accused: the black mole, shaped like a baby's hand, on the left side of his neck. Because I haven't seen a photograph of her, his victim remains a blank in my memory bank.

During the trial, very little was said about her. The whole exciting courtroom drama revolved around her executioner.

# The Birth and Death of
# the Miracle Man

The second school term was over.

Fiasola Ta'ase, the head teacher at Sapepe, went round and made sure all the doors and windows of his four-teacher school were locked. Even the teachers had gone home, and the building breathed a steady, healing silence. Some children, who were playing marbles under the breadfruit trees behind the school, scattered home when they saw him.

Back in his classroom he rolled a cigarette and sat smoking it at his desk. He had lived in Sapepe for twenty years, and, in that time, had married Filifili, daughter of one of Sapepe's leading aiga, had sired four sons and four daughters and had developed what the Chief Inspector of Schools had referred to, a month before in a meeting of head teachers, as 'the best school in Upolu'. He was also a senior deacon.

His clothes were damp with sweat, so he stripped off his shirt, spread it out on the front desk, and fanned himself with an exercise book. Not long after, he heard footsteps hurrying along the concrete veranda outside his classroom.

Sieni, his second daughter, stood in the doorway. 'Filifili says you should come home now – your food is cooked.' Without looking at her, he nodded once. She left immediately.

He flicked his cigarette butt out of the nearest window. Their fale across the malae looked empty; a rippling sea of heat waves was brimming out of its corrugated iron roof.

His lunch – boiled bananas and tinned fish – was on a food-mat in the middle of the fale. There was no one about. He sat down cross-legged and, after saying a short grace, started eating.

'Now you can rest for two weeks,' Filifili said when she came and sat down a few yards away. 'Is there anything you want the children to do during the holidays?'

He pushed his food-mat away and placed his hands palms upwards on his knees.

'Bring some washing water!' Filifili called to the kitchen fale.

Sieni brought a basin of water and a hand-towel. He washed his hands, dried them and she took the things away.

'Did we get a letter from Tavita?' Filifili asked. He shook his head. Tavita, the oldest of their children, had been living in New Zealand for nearly five years.

Filifili left for the kitchen fale to eat with the rest of their aiga.

He sat staring at the malae which was bristling with the fierce afternoon light.

After showering, he dressed in a clean lavalava and T-shirt, sat in his favourite wooden chair facing the road, and gazed through the gaps between the dwellings on the shore at the sea quivering in the evening light. Sometimes cars dug through the thickening gloom and made him think of strange creatures with enormous luminous eyes swimming through the depths of a dark ocean. His seven-year-old son, Malama, came and sat in his lap. He nestled him against his chest; Malama's hair smelled of coconut oil. Soon everything was throbbing to the incessant crying of cicadas.

After the women had strung up the mosquito nets, Malama joined the other children in the largest net, and

Fiasola listened to their chatter and laughter until they fell asleep one by one. Sieni lowered the fale blinds but left up the two rows in front of him. His skin tingled as the breeze rippled across it like the caress of soft hands, and he remembered how, as a boy, he had observed his grandmother and another old woman bathing his father's corpse in a tub of water, drying it carefully, and then rubbing coconut oil into the corpse's skin. The gold ring round the middle finger of his grandmother's left hand had shone brilliantly in the lamp-light as her fearless hands had massaged his father's body with oil until it had glistened.

Filifili turned down the lamp and the darkness invaded their fale immediately. 'Shall I turn it right off?' she asked. He didn't reply so she left the light as it was and got into their mosquito net. Shortly after, he was surveying the mosquito nets that filled the fale. They glowed dimly in the half-light and reminded him of huge butterfly cocoons. The crying of the cicadas had ceased, and now, at the tip of his hearing, was the muffled swishing of the surf washing over the reef.

An hour or so later, he lay down beside Filifili, clasped his hands on his chest, and stared up into the dark dome of the net. He couldn't escape her smell of coconut oil or the sound of her breathing. He closed his eyes and imagined the darkness to be a hungry dog biting at its flea-infested body, its teeth clicking.

He jerked awake and sat up.

Filifili rolled over and faced him. 'Is anything the matter?' she whispered. Lying down again, he turned his back to her.

He forced himself to stay awake all night.

Before anyone else was up, he changed into a working lavalava, got his bush-knife, and hurried to their plantation where, all day, he weeded his taro patch. That night, after everyone fell asleep, he sat in his chair. He thought he could hear the faint scratching of claws on the parched ground and the humming of the wings of flying foxes, as the night's chill set in.

He stayed awake all that night, and the next, and the next.

On the fifth day of the holidays, he and his sons picked the ripe cacao fruit in their plantation. (The cacao beans, when dry, would be sold and the money used to pay his children's school fees.) The darkness that night was empty even of memories. Gradually he heard the soft moaning and purring of women, and, as he concentrated on it, the women pressed in around him; soon their musky odour was invading him through his pores. With the odour came nausea; he tried to lie as still as stone but the trembling that was emanating from the agitated pool of his loins started to break in spasmodic waves through his body. He rolled out of the net and hurried out of the fale.

'Are you ill?' Filifili asked him during their Saturday morning meal. He shook his head. She sprang up and left. He watched her until she disappeared into the kitchen fale.

After his sons finished eating, he helped them wash the raw cacao beans and tie them up in baskets to ferment for a few days. Then they got firewood and foodstuffs for their Sunday umu from their plantation. In the afternoon he lay on his stomach in the main fale, and watched his sons and their friends playing cricket on the malae. One boy tripped on the concrete pitch and cut open his left knee. Fiasola noticed that the blood wove like a thin eel down the boy's leg. When he saw Filifili approaching the fale, he hurried to his classroom, where he stayed until evening smoking at his desk and scrutinizing the rows of empty desks and the walls and blackboards and the charts, notices and drawings on them. He kept returning to the small pencil drawing which Malama had drawn and pinned on the bottom right-hand corner of the back wall. It was of an octopus with fifteen legs and one black, unblinking eye in the centre of its head. The corners of the drawing had curled up, and the octopus appeared to be trapped in a shallow pit.

Filifili was still waiting for him when he got into their net just after midnight. 'What is the matter?' she began. 'I have to know.' No reply. 'You eat hardly anything; you stay awake nearly all night; you refuse to talk to anyone – not even to your children. What have we done wrong?' When he maintained his silence, she started crying softly into the end of her sleeping-sheet. He put an arm round her and pressed her against him.

A short while later, he watched himself making love to her.

She fell asleep soon after.

Everything had stopped growing. A large stone altar stood in the centre of the stillness. On it was Malama, naked, his arms and legs tied together with strips of bark. All around them, he sensed a huge crowd watching, avidly anticipating his every move. Someone, who had pastor Simi's voice, shouted: 'Kill him, kill the ungrateful son!' He moved towards Malama. His son screamed, his bleeding fingers tearing at the stone. Fiasola ordered his feet to stop following each other; they refused. Suddenly he was gazing up into a sky ablaze with a half-moon. Then the moon like a blade was in his hand and plunging down at Malama's throat. The blade vanished from his hand; his hands were tightening round the boy's throat, and he was weeping, unable to unclasp his hands. There was loud cheering and clapping.

He was sobbing when he awoke to his two eldest sons pinning back his arms, and Filifili clutching her throat and gasping for breath. It was daylight. He tore through the net and fled towards the safety of the plantations.

'Fiasola, don't go away!' he heard Malama call. He crouched in the middle of a thick clump of fau trees. Dewdrops covered the vegetation; in the morning light, they twinkled like tears.

When he heard his sons searching for him, he emerged from his hiding place. Malama took his hand. On their way home, his sons talked to him as if nothing had happened.

'Filifili is all right,' Malama whispered to him as they neared their kitchen fale, where Filifili and the rest of their aiga were making the umu. 'It was only a bad dream, wasn't it, Fiasola?' asked Malama. He nodded once. The air was dizzy with smoke and the acrid smell of burning wood. He remembered it was Sunday.

He didn't attend any of the church services, and, early that night, with a light wind weaving lazily through the village, he went to consult Simi, their pastor and his most trusted friend.

They sat in chairs facing the road, without speaking for a long time.

'Tell me about it,' Simi said finally.

'Something is happening to me, and I don't understand it.' Fiasola paused and looked at his friend. Simi was descended from Solomon Islanders, and, in the gloom, his blackness was the solidity of black river boulders. 'It is as if God has forsaken me but I do not care. As if everything and everyone is of no importance any more; that even if the people I cherish pass away or are killed I will feel nothing. I am not even frightened that I feel this. I am strangely fascinated by it.'

'You are exaggerating, Fiasola. Think carefully. You love your aiga, and love means caring about what happens to them . . .'

'There is no meaning in prayer any more. My position as a deacon is meaningless also. So are most of the things which up to now gave me value . . .'

'Don't you care about what happens to your wife and children? What about the school you have spent all your working life building up? And this village, *our* village, which we both came to as strangers but have helped to turn into the most prosperous in Samoa? Yes, and our friendship, what about that?'

40

Fiasola found himself walking towards the front steps of the house. 'I have to go.'

'Wait!' Simi called.

Turning slowly, Fiasola said, 'It is all right. I *was* exaggerating. God is still with me.' Quickly, he walked down the steps before Simi could say anything else.

On his slow way home, he admitted to himself that someone was being born inside him. This had been revealed to him while he had been talking to Simi, and he hadn't wanted to tell Simi about it.

'Tauilopepe sent word last night that he wants to see you this morning,' Filifili told him on Monday morning as he was putting on his working clothes. Tauilopepe was Chairman of the School Committee, and the most power-ful and richest Sapepe ali'i. 'He said it was important.' Whenever Tauilopepe had wanted to see him, he had gone promptly, but now, instead of doing that, he picked up his bush-knife and headed towards the plantations. 'What shall I tell Tauilopepe?' Filifili called.

Malama ran up and walked beside his father.

As they climbed over the high rock fence behind their kitchen fale, Fiasola noticed, above the heads of the palm trees ahead, that rain clouds were massing on the mountain range.

'It is my birthday,' he said. 'I am forty-nine today.'

'That's very old, eh?' Malama asked. Fiasola nodded.

Mid-morning, while he planted taro, the rain broke in a running clatter. Malama sheltered under some nearby banana trees and watched him from there. Fiasola stuck his oso into the soft ground, leaned on it with both hands and allowed the cool rain, which grew heavier, to wash over him.

He started to sleep. Malama rushed out and led him into the small fale in the middle of the plantation, where he spread out some mats and told him to sleep there. Fiasola shook his head repeatedly but was forced to lie down when he started shivering almost uncontrollably. Malama covered him with other mats. Within a short while, he was asleep, his snoring lost in the rain's loud beat.

'You must not tell your mother,' he instructed Malama on the way home.

'That it is your birthday?'

'Never mind.'

'She should know anyway, eh?'

After their evening lotu, Filifili reminded him about Tauilopepe. On his way to Tauilopepe's, he veered off the road and sat on the church steps.

At dawn he returned home without having seen Tauilopepe, and fell into a deep slumber. When Filifili woke in the morning, she instructed their aiga not to disturb him. He slept all day, with the lulling patter of the rain echoing at the edge of his dreams.

They woke him for the evening meal. He ate hungrily, then occupied his chair and observed the rain tumbling through the darkness. He went to sleep at dawn and slept the whole day.

He was unusually cheerful during their evening meal, talking and laughing with his children. When the others had gone to bathe, he spoke to Filifili for the first time in over a week.

'A miracle man is being born inside me in my sleep, in my dreaming,' he explained eagerly. 'He refuses to be born if I sleep at night. Only in my daytime sleep and dreaming does he take more and more visible shape. So I must not sleep at night. You must help me do that, Filifili.' Paused. 'Soon I will understand all that is happening.' He went and sat in his chair.

'Why don't you go and see Simi? He will explain everything to you,' she pleaded.

'Simi is God's man; he is not my man.'

'What about seeing Tauilopepe then?'

'He belongs to Power and Wealth.'

She walked over on her knees and sat at his feet.

'I can feel it, Filifili. Soon he will be born and he will explain everything to me.'

'What is there to understand?' she asked. He looked puzzled. 'What, Fiasola?' He reached down and clasped her hands. She tried not to cry as she gazed into his dazzling eyes.

Late that night, with Filifili watching over him and the rain falling as if it was never going to stop, he fell asleep in his chair without meaning to, and, in his dreaming, he slit the miracle man's throat with the half-moon, stretched him out on the stone altar, and then watched his grandmother's hands, the gold ring on her left hand aglitter with tears, oiling the miracle man's body with the crimson blood that was weaving in eel-like rivulets from his throat. The miracle man, he noted nonchalantly, wore his face. He marched triumphantly out of his dreaming into his classroom of wildly applauding pupils; even the octopus in Malama's drawing on the back wall was clapping loudly with all its fifteen legs.

# Elena's Son

I make friends easy. My mother she say I have God's gift for to love all kinds of people.

It start for to rain heavy as the bus stop in front of Sapepe church. I get out and the wind it whip the cold rain into me and I am soaking wet before you can blink your eye. I not know where Tupu's house is. Tupu he is my mother's oldest brother and the main matai of our Sapepe aiga. Never before have I been in Sapepe but I hear it is the most rich village in Samoa. The wind it push the rain across everything. The rain it shake and shiver and whip like a bad temper. Through it I see that Sapepe it got more palagi houses than other villages. The church it is nearly as big as the Apia Mulivai Cathedral.

No one around to ask, so I run to the next house and poke the wet head through the doorway and ask the women who are weaving mats there. They just shake the head. I run to the next house and the next and the next but no luck. I remember Tupu he has another matai name, so in the next house I use that name and the people they point to the other end of Sapepe and they say that Tupu he live next to the school. I now am shivering bad. My skin it is all shrivel up like that of the old man, so I run fast. My feet they go squish and squash and squish in the mud and sand. I begin for to feel sorry that I have come and when I see Tupu's home

44

my sorriness it get worse. It is only two fale and in the rain
they look like old and hungry dogs. They even look worse
because they are surrounded by big palagi houses. I wonder why Tupu he not have a big house too.

The main fale it has all the blinds down. I rush up to
the back paepae and lift some blinds. The smell of sweat
like the smell of the flying fox it hit me at once. I try not
to breathe.

A large woman, and I know she is Taimane the wife
of Tupu, has a girl in her lap and she is looking for utu
in the girl's hair. Near them there is some boys playing
cards. They make little noise. At the other end there
sleep an old man with his head on the ali, and he is
snoring. All who are awake they stop everything and
look at me. I stoop the self and walk in and sit down
against one of the back posts. My clothes they at once
start for to drip the wetness into the mat. I expect
someone to greet me. No one do it. They all look at the
man who is mending the fishing net by the bed. In the
shadow he is. His wife Taimane she call to him, someone
has come. He continue for to work and not look up. Yes,
it is Elena's son, you give him something for to eat, he
say. I am really surprised that he know who I am. You
see I never meet him before. Taimane and her daughter
they go out for to get me food. The boys they continue
their card game. The old man he snore on.

How is your mother, Tupu he ask me. She is well
thank you, I lie to him. I no tell him that my mother she
no longer with me as she gone to another village with
her third husband. That is good, Tupu he say. Just then
Taimane she return and throw a dry lavalava to me and
she point to the curtain. I go for to change behind the
curtain.

When I am seated again on the floor, the warm it start
for to embrace me.

It is good you have come, this is your home, Tupu he
say. I bring nothing, I reply. Tupu he just smile.

His children they come and sit with me and we play

45

cards. Soon I am laughing and joking with them. Later, after I eat, we go to the kitchen fale and cook the evening meal. It rain and rain but I am no longer sorry for coming to my Sapepe aiga. As Tupu say already to me, this is my home.

I soon find out that Tupu and Taimane and the other elders in our aiga they don't say much between themself. They seem for to understand each other without too much talk. All the young people they obey them and know what to do without getting orders. Sometime Taimane she has to smack some of the naughty children and Tupu he tell us off during lotu if we disobey the elders. But everybody they do their work well. I too soon fit into that. However under all this peace I feel that something is wrong. Tupu and Taimane and all my Sapepe relatives they never talk about the past like there is too much pain there. No one in Sapepe speak of it either. I note other things too. Our aiga it is the only one in Sapepe that don't have a big plantation.

All the other aiga they have cocoa and copra plantations that get them enough money for to build palagi houses and send some of their children to school in Apia. Also all of them they have relatives living in New Zealand who send them money. The Tauilopepe aiga it is the most rich aiga in Sapepe. Tauilopepe he own the Leaves of the Banyan Tree Plantation that cover half of the Sapepe land and go right up to the top of the mountain range. He got trucks and stores and shares in many Apia business too. The Sapepe church it is mainly a memorial to his son Pepe who no one is allowed to speak about if Tauilopepe is about. Like everybody in Sapepe, Tauilopepe he treat Tupu and our aiga kindly. Everytime Taimane she send me to Tauilopepe's store to get some goods I notice that the person who serve me never put down the cost in our account. It is like Tauilopepe he is paying Tupu back for a great debt.

*

Children's Sunday it is the most important Sunday
in Samoa and it is a week before it, and our aiga it need
some money for to get new white clothes for the
children. Tauilopepe he has many people from nearby
villages for to work on his plantation. Me and three of
Tupu's sons we are told by Taimane for to go work for
Tauilopepe. On Monday morning we get on the trucks
at Tauilopepe's store and in one half hour we stop at
the cocoa drier in the middle of the plantation where
Ta'ifau, who run the plantation, he divide us into
gangs. All the gangs they are run by Ta'ifau's sons. Muga
he is our overseer.

No shelter from the sun. It is burning into our heads.
We weed the area of cocoa. Muga he set a fast pace.
Never before do I do this hard work and I nearly give
up but I see my cousins not giving up so I keep going.
Muga he suddenly come to me and tell me for to get
water for everyone and all that morning I am the water-
carrier. I wonder why Muga he pick on me for to do this
easy work. At noontime we rest in the shade and eat
boiled bananas and ta'amu and a stew of tinned fish.
One hour later, we start work again. After three days, I
find the self it is all in pain and my skin it is all burnt
but I keep it up. The plantation I forget for to tell you is
called after the biggest banyan tree in Sapepe. Everybody they call it The Tree and it is in the centre of the
plantation. When we rest at noontime on the third day
I finish my meal quick and go up for to look at the Tree
and the fale under it in which live Faito'aga and his
aiga. Faito'aga he is Tauilopepe's most trusted relative
and most Sapepe people are afraid of him because they
say he is afraid of nobody.

The roots of the Tree they are like the arms and legs
of a giant. All around the roots there are flying hundreds
of moths and insects. They are like dancing thoughts.
They dance here and dance there in the air. The shade
it is so cool and it smell of rich life growing all the time.
I sit the self on a root that crawl along the ground and

look up at the leaves and branches. Suddenly there is a young boy beside me. He got long hair like the girl and he wear no clothes. My father he say for you to come and eat with us, he say. Tell your father no thank you, I reply in politeness. He say you must come, he say. So I follow him to their fale at the other end of the Tree's roots.

Already Faito'aga his wife and children they are eating in a circle in their fale. This is not usual. The custom it say that the head of the aiga he should not eat with women or children. I enter through the back. Faito'aga he wave to me for to sit opposite to him between two of his sons. I do so. Faito'aga he point to the food in front of me. The others they just look at me one time and then continue eating. Faito'aga he do the same so I join them. Nobody talk. There is only the sound of chewing and swallowing and sucking and the buzzing of the flies. When Faito'aga finish eating and he is washing his hands in the basin he ask, you staying with Tupu. I nod the head. Tupu he is my good friend but I not seen him much for a long time, he say. Since all that trouble, his wife begin for to say but Faito'aga he look hard at her and she stop talking.

As we walk back to work, Faito'aga he say, you tell Tupu you met me and you come and eat with us every day. Thank you very much, I reply. He start for to walk away then he stop and ask, is Elena your mother. I nod the head and then watch him walk off. He is not a big man but he walk through the shade of the Tree like he own everything. That evening as I help Tupu drag our canoe up from the beach I tell him I had a meal with Faito'aga. He is my friend, he save me once, Tupu he say. I want him for to say some more but he don't.

All that week I eat at noontime with Faito'aga and his aiga. How much schooling you have, he ask me. I tell him I been up to standard six. On Friday, me and my cousins we get paid. We give the money to Taimane for the children's Sunday. On Monday, I ask Tupu if I can go on working for Tauilopepe. We not need the money but, if you want to, then you do it, he say. At work Muga he tell me that Faito'aga he want me for to work with him. I am puzzled but am happy about it. I get to Faito'aga's fale and find Ta'ifau there with him. Everyone is afraid of Ta'ifau. He is a no-nonsense man and is in charge of Tauilopepe's business. This is Elena's son, Faito'aga he tell Ta'ifau, who smile at me and ask, Faito'aga he tell me you can write and add figures and read some English. I nod the head. So he give to me an exercise book and a ballpoint pen and say for me to come with Faito'aga and him. I am to write down everything they tell me for to write down. We go in this jeep and spend all morning inspecting the plantation. Never do they tell me anything for to write down. For a week I go everywhere with them but my exercise book remain empty.

At noontime Friday, we drive up to Faito'aga's fale. My heart it beat fast as I see who is there. It is Tauilopepe and it is the first time I see him up close. Ta'ifau he join him at the front and they eat while Faito'aga and me and everybody serve them. The two old men they talk like we are not there. Tauilopepe he talk slowly because there is something wrong in his speaking. He look older than Ta'ifau. His hair it is nearly all grey and he wear the sunglasses all the time, and his right arm it is dead, and when he walk he drag his right leg slightly. A result of a stroke, I hear. This is Elena's son, Ta'ifau he tell Tauilopepe after they eat. I bow the head when I feel Tauilopepe look at me through his black glasses. He look very strong, Tauilopepe he say. And he had a good schooling, Ta'ifau he say. And he is a hard worker and will make a good overseer, Faito'aga he say. So you two train him and get him for to learn how to run the store too, Tauilopepe he say. I feel I got no say in what they decide, so I just sit. Ta'ifau, you talk to Tupu about it, Tauilopepe he say. From my eye corner, I see that Ta'ifau he not look like he want for to do that and I am puzzled some more. After lotu that night I tell Tupu what Tauilopepe want me to do. He just nod the head like it is not important.

About one week after I start overseer training, I see that Tupu and Taimane they are talking more between themself. They also give orders to our aiga. No hurtful orders are said, but the talk it get more. I am pleased, for now I talk with the elders and especially with Tupu. He even play cards with us young people at night. As our aiga start for to talk more so do the Sapepe people. However I never ask anybody for to tell me the secret pain that is in the past of my aiga. I feel it is no business of mine. I work hard and halfway through the year I begin for to help overseer the gangs. I also spend two days per week working with Ta'ifau in Tauilopepe's house and we check the business books. Tauilopepe he sometime work with us and I find that he has the fast brain with figures though he had little schooling. One morning he just sit and watch me and Ta'ifau. He been drinking the night before. I can smell it. He don't move and I am trapped in the stare of his black glasses. You know your father, he ask me. I shake the head. His name it was Maluelue and he was not of Sapepe, he say. Ta'ifau and me we stop working. He was from Malaelua, Ta'ifau he say. I know that too. My mother she tell me. I sweat under their stare. Your mother tell you how Maluelue died, Tauilopepe he ask me. I nod the head once. She tell you what kind of man he was, he ask. I nod again. Tell me, he order. I can't speak. Don't be afraid, he say. She tell me he was a good tufuga, sir, I reply. Yes, but what kind of man, he ask. Sir, he was good and kind and he loved God, I reply. He do not know, eh, Tauilopepe he say to Ta'ifau. Tauilopepe he rise slowly and shuffle out. I wait for Ta'ifau for to tell me the truth but he don't. It is like the wild rain of the day I arrived in Sapepe is still inside me, and, if I don't find out the truth, the rain inside will shrivel me up.

That night I play cards with Tupu. Everybody they

are asleep. Sir, you know I never knew my father Maluelue, I say to him. Was he a good man? I ask. Yes, he a good man and he loved your mother, he reply. He was here nearly one year. Your mother was in Malaelua staying with our relatives and he made her his wife and they shifted here for to stay. The accident that killed him happened about eleven months later. This is Tupu's story and I believe him. The next evening I hear Tupu and Taimane arguing for the first time. They do not know I am listening to the last bit of their talk. He must go before everything that happened come back to destroy us, she tell him. No, he say. I know they are referring to me.

Some evenings I work late at the store and Tauilopepe or his wife Lupe they ask me for to stay the night. I refuse politely at first but then, as I go home and feel my relatives they are suffering because of me, I stay at Tauilopepe's home more and more. If I work on the plantation I stay with Faito'aga and his aiga. But always I go home on Sunday. Everytime I am there I feel Tupu and Taimane they are suffering worse and worse. Also I feel they do not want me for to leave really. It is like they want my presence because it is the punishment for some great sin they have committed. When I am away from them, I hear from people that they are quarrelling many times.

I don't know what to do, until one night a cousin he rush to the store and he tell me that Tupu he is in the hospital with the serious illness. I run to the hospital. On the bed he is asleep. Taimane is beside the bed crying. The doctor he tell me Tupu will be all right. It is only a small heart attack. But Tupu he now look old all of a sudden. It is only one week since I saw him last but he is an old man now. When Taimane see me she turn away like she is afraid of me. I hurry away. I have to know. That night I walk in the darkness to Faito'aga's fale. The darkness it hold me like a fist.

Faito'aga he is cleaning the shotgun. His aiga they are

asleep. I enter. He see me. He point opposite him. I sit down. Why am I to be the one to tell you, he ask me. Because Tupu he is your true friend, I reply. He put the shotgun under the bed. You will do nothing bad after I tell you, he ask. I nod the head. He look at me for a long time then he say straight out, Tupu he killed your father when they go fishing. He stop. I feel nothing. He continue. Tupu he killed him because it had to be done. Tupu he was very ill when he returned from the fishing. I bring him here and make him well again. Tauilopepe he get a doctor for to live here and look after him. In his illness he tell me everything. He tell Ta'ifau and Tauilopepe too. Your father's body it was never found. Tupu he killed him with a spear and tied the body to some coral. It was what all the elders wanted for to happen to Maluelue. Tupu he knew that and he carried it out. He loved your mother and he had to protect the honour of your aiga. What he did we all agree was proper. But Tupu he had for to live with it for twenty years. All of us in Sapepe we tried for to protect him from the pain. We thought he was over it but you bring it all back.

When Maluelue return to Sapepe with your mother at first he impress everybody with his skill. He build many fale for Sapepe people. However, for no reason known, he start for to beat your mother. Not in public at first, but it get more public as it happen more often. Tupu he does nothing for to stop him. Your father even start for to accuse your mother of going with other men. He himself start for to go with other women and he don't bother for to keep them a secret. He disappear with one woman and we all hope he don't return but he does. For a while he behave all right. Then when your mother is carrying you the beating it start again. He again go with other women and the disgrace on your aiga is heavy. Some men of your aiga threaten for to stop him but Tupu he say no. Maluelue he even tell everyone that Tupu is a coward who is too afraid to punish him. Then Tauilopepe and the Council they rule that Tupu must control Maluelue and, if not, the Council will send Maluelue out of Sapepe. Tupu he does nothing until the day he find out that a woman of another aiga is with your father's child. The rest I told you already. Tupu he had to do it.

Before Faito'aga can say anything else I get up and leave his fale. The darkness it is no longer the fist that trap me. I breathe easy and walk slow. I hate no one. Not Tupu. Not my father. Not my mother. I am to blame too. When I formed in my mother's womb I become the final cause of the destruction of my parents and the pain of Tupu.

It is dawn as I walk to the next village for to catch the bus to Apia. Tupu he will wake up this morning in the hospital and he will find my letter and read it. I hope what I have written in it will ease his pain.

In Apia I will catch the bus to the village of my father where I will stay with my relatives for to find out more about my father and why he was an evil man. As I say, already people tell me I have God's gift for to love all kinds of people. Perhaps I can learn for to love my father too.

# Exam Failure Praying

Make the prayer, my father tell me last night at our aiga lotu, so I make the prayer and say to God our Father, you look after us tonight and so on. I am good at the prayers because, since I was a tiny boy, my father he get me and my brothers and my sisters and my cousins for to learn how to make the prayers. He also get us for to read from the Holy Book until now I am sixteen years old and am the expert in the reading of the Book. My father he always tell us that the prayer is always a help to us for to pass our exams in school. He instruct us for to pray before every exam, so from primer one at our Sapepe school I pray and up through the standards and up to form four the Catholic high school, St Josephs. My father he don't like the Roman Church but he arrange for me to go schooling there because I don't get good enough marks at form two for to go into a government high school. He really want me for to go to Samoa College where all the clever students go, but I fail and it is the first time I disgrace my father and my aiga. This time I commit the second disgrace. Last month I sit the form four exam and even with all my prayers I still fail it and now I am too afraid for to tell my father and my aiga. Last night I was going for to tell him but I do not get enough courage from God for to do it. The form four exam it is very important, because if you do not pass it you are not allowed into form five and so on. All day today I spend in our plantation and pretend for to work. I am so afraid and lost for what to do. I am a disgrace. My father he spend all his money and life trying for to get me through school and here I am a failure. My father tell us that in Samoa if you do not have a good education you go nowhere and get no job or even go to New Zealand to earn much money. My father he want me for to be a government scholarship student and go to New Zealand and become a lawyer. It is the desire of every father in Samoa for their sons to do this. In my aiga only my cousin Uili he is able to go to New Zealand on the scholarship but he only return as a plumber with the palagi wife who soon get sick of the village life and go back home with their two children. I am the oldest so my father expect me for to pass everything and be the good example to the young ones. But here I am the failure. Perhaps I shall go and hang myself like that other boy in Salamumu I read about in the *Samoa Times*. Perhaps I shall go and drink poison weed-killer like that other boy in Vaivase who I read about too. But there is still hope in the prayers. I shall keep praying to God for to enter into my father's heart and make him forgive me when I tell him about my failure. If our loving God He does that for me, I will try for to pass the entering exam into Malua Theological College and study for to be a pastor like my uncle Samani who is very loved and respected by his village, Savaia. Samani he never been to high school but he still pass Malua College so with the help of God and my humble prayers to Him I too can pass and become a Man of God. If I become that I am sure my father and aiga they will all love me because being a Man of God is more worthy than becoming a lawyer. Tonight at our aiga lotu I hope for to receive enough courage from our Loving Father for to tell my father and aiga about my failure and the bad disgrace I have again brought to them. If I do not get the courage I do not know what I am going to do.

# The Balloonfish and the Armadillo

---

A lone cicada in the garden in front of your house is sucking at the night's succulent thickness; its rhythmic trilling picks at the silence, like the beating of your heart, while you sit at your desk in your study, a magazine open on your table, you pay it no attention, your skin covered with a cool film of sweat. The air is ponderous with humidity; every time you place your arms on your desk, your sweat stains it. All the bookshelves that wall your study are inhabited by books. Neat. Tidy. Expensive. Immaculate proof of your learning and success. Into this womb you retreat almost every night now.

Your wife is asleep in your bedroom at the other end of the house. For a moment you picture her, sheet drawn up to her neck, arms crossed over her ribs, her pale face shining like marble in the light of her bedside lamp, eyes shut, her breathing hardly audible. You've been married for thirty-five years and, always, she has slept in that position. Some nights, while watching her, you think she is dead or dying (or more frightening, lying on a sacrificial altar inviting the priest's stone knife). You've dared not tell her this. Recently, at a particularly boring cocktail party, you told everyone that she was still 'the passion of your life'. When you returned home she chastised you: 'You shouldn't get so drunk!' You refused to tell her that you hadn't touched a drop all night.

56

You break from your thoughts when you hear a mouse scratching at the ceiling directly above you. A quick, urgent scratching. Must get some rat poison.

It is after midnight. In the air, wafting in slowly from the veranda, you detect the odour of the dark-green moss that lives on the barks of the immense monkey-pod trees outside. A rich, medicinal scent that you enjoy. The mouse scratches again. You glance up, expecting to see tiny claws piercing the ceiling.

Yesterday was your sixty-first birthday. For ten years you have refused your wife's offer of birthday parties. Waste of money, you keep telling her. But you don't begrudge her the money spent on her grand birthday celebrations: orgies of food and drink and meaningless conversation and gossip, good for business, though.

You imagine the night is an enormous whale curled protectively around your house up on these slopes, a kindly, benevolent softness into which you can sink, be embraced by. Your son John, who everyone fears as the relentlessly honest and righteous Attorney General, and Nora, his humourless New Zealand wife, whose charity extends to running the newly formed Society for the Intellectually Handicapped, and their two teenage sons, thoroughly spoilt demanders of everything and who respect nothing, came for your birthday dinner last night. You've never been able to think of Nora as your daughter-in-law, and her sons as your grandchildren. To keep them at a distance you give them anything they want. Your wife knows the way you feel about them; you never provide her with the opportunity to discuss it though. Whenever they visit, the conversation, the warmth and rapport is always with your son only. Nora and her sons keep trying to break into the sacred circle but you always ease them out of it politely, firmly.

Your T-shirt, now drenched with sweat, sticks to your body; it feels like a slippery second skin. You get up, peel it off, drop it into the wastepaper basket, walk over to the open windows and, hands on your hips, you let the faint breeze caress your skin with its cool fingers. Soon the acrid smell of your own body invades your nostrils. You suck it in deeply and hold it down. One . . . two . . . three – you count to fifteen and then ease the air out of your lungs. Your own smell reminds you suddenly of a woman's sap during sexual intercourse. You don't expect a pleasurable reaction from your flesh, and you don't get it. You fondle yourself slowly, deliberately tempting the once almost uncontrollable passions of your flesh. No reaction. It is good, you tell yourself. You live beyond physical desire now. Free of it.

At the edge of the light cast from the windows of your study, the night walks. You think of it as your son, in flowing silk-black robes, pacing the shadow of the Judge's bench, defiantly stalking the guilty, the sinners, the innocent . . .

Last Monday night while I was in my study my recurring migraine grew to inhabit, almost to bursting, the whole of my head, and, as usual, I tried to ignore the intense pain.

I have always pictured my migraine as a fully inflated balloonfish with its spikes extended like threatening spears, bulbous eyes staring unblinkingly at me, its small round mouth opening and shutting in time to its breathing, suspended in the still sun-clear waters of a tropical reef. Why I came to associate this creature with my migraine, I'll never be able to fathom. I can remember though that my migraine first roared out of the depths of my brain the night I watched, with a mixture of horror and fascination, my son being born in Auckland Hospital where my wife, who doesn't trust the local hospital, had insisted on going. All babies, so the stereotype goes, are expected to scream as they are slapped for the first time by the hostile cold of our atmosphere. John's reaction, however, was an unforgiving, contemptuous silence, and, in his eyes, I caught an accusation. He seemed an utterly self-contained being from another planet. Perhaps the round accusing silence of the balloonfish reflected John's birth silence. But even suffering the first full impact of my migraine, my eyes brimmed with tears of joy: the love I felt then for my son was greater than I had experienced for anyone and anything else before. I would tell no one, not even my wife, of how I had felt then, nursing my treasure secretly, afraid that if I revealed it to anyone it would diminish in value.

That night while I foraged in my desk drawers for the flask of brandy to drug my migraine, I rediscovered the folder of papers which my father had left me almost twelve years before when he had died of a stroke, and which I had avoided looking at.

My father, who was nearly ninety when he died, was a self-made man (so he was described in business circles). His parents were humble villagers, so, after pastor's school, at the age of fourteen, he was apprenticed to a German carpenter, and, with his very meagre wage, he supported his parents and six brothers and sisters. He discovered early that to succeed in business in Apia he would have to learn German and English and accounting. He proceeded to master these at night by teaching himself and, during the day, by practising on his employer and any other person who was fluent in English or German. In 1914, he put his knowledge into effective use when the Germans were expelled from Samoa by the English-speaking New Zealanders, and he took over the German carpenter's modest construction business. Throughout his life he was admired, even by his business rivals, for his impeccable English, business acumen, and his inspired sermons as a lay preacher in the English-speaking Protestant Church where he met and married my mother, against her parents' wishes.

Proud of his 'self-creation and self-education', his own description, he refused to throw away anything, especially the literature, which he collected or generated. His spaciously gloomy bedroom came to be stacked on one side, from floor to ceiling, with his treasure of boxes, cartons and crates containing all the books, magazines, papers and the other odds and ends of his education. It was as if he needed all this to prove to himself that he was an educated man. We were forbidden to touch any of it. I was tempted to but after Max, my oldest brother, suffered a severe beating for doing so, I dared not. Often, as a boy, I imagined the stack growing larger and larger, bursting out of the bedroom and filling all the other rooms, then the whole house, even the toilet, and eventually, with a loud thunder-like cracking, the house bursting apart and my father's treasure set out to smothering our country.

My father's hoard remained intact in his cavern-like bedroom right throughout his two marriages, his rise to being described in the papers as a 'prominent businessman', until the week after his funeral when my son and I went to examine it. (He had bequeathed it to me in his will. I was the only surviving son from his first marriage but he had five children by his second wife. I was puzzled, therefore, about his reason for leaving it to me, saying, in his will, that I deserved it.)

At that time my son, John, was a strapping nineteen-year-old who had just returned for the holidays, having graduated from high school (my old school in Auckland) and who was now getting ready to return to start law school in New Zealand.

My stepmother and her family were conveniently absent from the house which is situated on the banks of a stream of brackish water, known in the neighbourhood as the Vaipe, behind the Apia Police Station. It is a two-storeyed wooden building with rows of louvre windows, dark blue and green outside walls and a bright red roof. As tidy and neat as my father had always been. I was reluctant to visit it, fearing my father's hoard and the childhood memories that would entangle me once

I was there. Yet I also wanted, with an insatiable curiosity, to explore the mystery that my father had assumed in my life, after he had divorced my mother when I was twelve years old. In the entrails of that treasure, I hoped to find the father I never knew.

I hesitated at the front door of the house. Glanced at my son, a splendid youth on the threshold of discovering more about his grandfather. He smiled at me. We stepped into the house together.

In the sitting room I recognized nothing from my childhood. A TV set, an orderly array of expensively padded furniture, sea-green carpet, a garish velvet mural of the Last Supper; alone on the far wall was a large black and white photograph, framed in gold, of my father as a young man, in a stiff black suit, white shirt and bow tie, bowler hat in his right hand clasped to his belly. For a moment my breath stuck in my chest: my son was the mirror image of his grandfather, and, suddenly envious of the resemblance, I tried not to accept it. At John's age I had looked like my mother – short, stumpy, fair almost like a European, with brown, blond-tipped hair. Here, beside me, my father was alive again physically in the darkly handsome, very Samoan form of my son.

As we walked up the wooden stairs, I tried to suppress my inexplicable jealousy. Our footsteps rang hollow; the house smelled of the uncanny twists of history. 'How many times have you been here?' I asked my son in English. (In our home, as in my grandparents' home where I was reared, Samoan was spoken only to the servants and those Samoans who couldn't speak English.)

'I used to come on his birthdays, you know that.' My father's birthdays were only for his grandchildren: lavish organized games and presents and unlimited food for the children, while he sipped expensive whisky and observed them.

My father's bedroom was at the end of the dimly lit corridor. 'I've never been in there!' John whispered.

'It's been a long time for me,' I admitted. (Almost a lifetime, I wanted to say.)

'I liked him,' he said. 'I liked him a lot even though I visited him only once a year.' He paused. I wanted him to continue telling me about the man my father had grown into. John knew more about that man than I did. 'He kept telling us about you: how we, his grandchildren, should behave like you did as a boy. Obedient, hardworking, outstanding at school. How you always used to protect your brothers and friends who were weaker than you . . .'

I didn't want to listen any more. I turned the door-handle and pushed open the bedroom door.

The gloom of the bedroom gaped at us. Out of it seeped my father's smell: the healthy, almost stale odour of hard work, thrift, clean Sunday sermons, and his working khaki shirts and trousers which he insisted on wearing until they were shiny with age and then he cherished them more. Mingled with this, underlying it like a river-bed, was the strong smell of mould and old books and mildewing paper.

Hesitantly I entered the room.

The curtains were drawn. A brilliant slit of light, from a gap in the curtains, cut across the darkness. In it, bright particles of dust were floating.

It was as if I had never left that cluttered room with its stacks, the enormous four-poster bed and its canopy of a tasselled mosquito net, and the oversized kapok mattress covered with a thick white sheet with embroidered lace edges; its wall of cupboards, in which he stored all the presents he received but never used.

'Are you okay?' John asked me. I nodded, straightened up and walked to the stacks, with my back turned firmly to him.

'Open the curtains,' I said.

The zipping of the curtain rings being pulled across

the metal rod was like the sharp slashing of a bush-knife through parched grass. For a moment the daylight blinded me but I refused to let my son see me shield my eyes.

'What are we going to do with all this?' he asked, gesturing at the stacks.

It jumped out of the depths of my being before I realized it. 'Burn most of it!' my voice said. Before he could argue with me, I started dragging a box into the middle of the room. 'We'll take them outside and burn whatever we don't want!'

'But . . .' he started insisting.

'Just do what I'm asking you!' I said. His eyes, for an instant, were bright with anger. 'It is of little use to us!' I pleaded, avoiding his eyes. 'Whatever books are in good condition we'll give to the public library.'

He picked up a tattered cardboard box that was bursting with magazines. Fat cockroaches scuttled out of it and vanished into the stacks as John brushed past me.

I stood listening to my only son's footsteps thumping down the corridor and then down the stairs, remembering, with fear and regret, the unforgiving thunder of my father's boots stamping out of our house after quarrelling loudly with my mother whenever he came home drunk and accused her, our family and God of feeding off his blood, every sacrificial ounce of it. To block out such disturbing memories I hugged two small boxes and, as spiders and cockroaches burst out of them and wriggled down my clothes and body, I stumbled out of the room, dripping insects that hit the floor and fled like the boyhood years I didn't want to trap me.

There is a shady stand of fau trees behind the house, at the edge of the stream. The fau were yellow with flowers, their leaves were turning brown, ready to be shed. I found a half forty-four-gallon drum in the garage, rolled it to the middle of the fau trees and, using dry twigs and branches, started a small fire in it. The smoke wafted up into my face.

I refused to allow my thoughts to analyse, dissect or argue with me. Quickly I sorted through my two boxes, mainly files and accounts from his business. I watched my hands flipping through the pages, my mind reading random figures and sentences, then screwing up the pages, I dropped them into the flames. The fire surged up greedily as I fed it.

The papers seemed to be alive as they squirmed and turned black and crumpled into white ash. At times, bits of black swirled up into the tangled branches of the trees or over to lie on the water like shattered pieces of a black mirror.

John kept bringing the boxes; he refused to look at me.

The next box contained newspapers and magazines. I didn't bother to read any of them. My hands ripped and tore and screwed up the pages.

The fire roared like wind blowing through a small tunnel. I became oblivious of time, caught in the fury of feeding my father's remains into the fire.

All the books that were in good condition I saved in the empty boxes. A random survey of the books' titles revealed that my father had avoided collecting fiction – no poetry, or novels, or plays, or stories. Most were about religion, mainly fundamentalist tracts; there was a large section of biography and autobiography, mainly about religious and business leaders. I counted three about John P. Rockefeller. Travel literature was plentiful too; most of it was about Europe which my father had never visited. Teach-yourself books about construction, architecture, book-keeping, accounting, astronomy, French, Russian, English, carpentry and other subjects featured well too.

I saved none of the magazines or newspapers. The magazines were nearly all religious (the *Watchtower*, the *Light of the Angel* and so on) and practical, related to his business.

Once I glanced up from my work to see the whole

tangle of trees aswirl with white smoke that brimmed up fiercely, like a vengeful joy, through the foliage and into the hungry sky.

John kept bringing the boxes.

We were now into business ledgers and account books, filled mainly with his neat figures and handwriting. Thick, bulky well-bound books. To rip them apart I had to open them, hold one side down with my foot, and pull upwards with my hands. The sharp-edged pages cut my hands often, but I didn't notice. Scattering the torn pages over the flames, I watched all the debts he had incurred, all the profits he had worked so diligently to make and all the losses, that had left their wrinkles on his brow and a perpetually complaining peptic ulcer in his disciplined stomach, turn into ash. Like my own orderly life, his had been determined, to a great extent, by the profit and the loss neatly recorded and balanced, year in and year out. Even his family had lived according to that tide.

For a few frightening minutes a set of pictures flicked through my mind as I observed the thick leather cover of a ledger squirming and writhing and shrivelling up in the fire, like human skin. A group of Nazi SS Officers in their black regalia and armbands, their eyes capturing the flames in a mad joy, around a fire in which books were burning; white flame bursting from the mouth of an oven into which a corpse was being pushed; a row of high black chimneys thrusting arrogantly into a grey sky . . .

'Are you all right?' My son saved me. I nodded. Throughout the day he would ask that periodically, and I would notice that he was throwing nothing into the fire: he was leaving the burning, the burial in fire, to me.

At midday, John asked if I wanted to go home for lunch. I shook my head and continued feeding the fire. Soon after, I realized that I hadn't come across any letters, so when I went through the boxes I looked for them. Their absence was a painful puzzle. Letters contained personal revelations but there were none, why?

'Have you come across any of his letters?' I asked John who shook his head. 'How far have we got?'

'About half-way through the mountain!' He chuckled.

We would find no letters to or from him. To me he had bequeathed an inheritance without eyes into his flesh, blood and spirit. Once again a deliberate denial, and I raged, working more intensely to thrust more and more of his corpse into the flames.

A few months after they divorced, my father married a woman who was almost half his age. We (my mother and two brothers Max and Henry) shifted to my mother's family, wealthy merchants who hadn't wanted her to marry 'that poor and uneducated Samoan' (my grandmother's description). They were half-castes (part-Europeans is the term in vogue) but considered themselves 'Europeans' superior to 'the Samoans'.

My grandfather's father had been an American trader from Connecticut who settled in Samoa, marrying my great-grandmother who was the daughter of another American trader and a Samoan mother. On the other hand, my mother's mother was the daughter of English missionaries.

My grandparents refused to allow us, their grandchildren, to see our father again; they did it effectively by sending us to St Andrews, an Anglican boarding school in Auckland, New Zealand; and in our presence they never again referred to our father or mentioned his name.

Even our Samoan surname was changed to our grandparents' English one. It was as though our father had never existed, that we had been 'born of a virgin' (Henry's description, later). Our mother never remarried; she had many suitors but, encouraged by her parents, she could never again break from the rich, comfortable bondage of her home.

My grandparents, though they were born and raised in Samoa and had visited America only once and England twice, modelled the life of our family on what they believed was that of the English Victorian gentry. Our lives were governed by the word *proper*. There was, said my stern and austere grandfather (whom I respected but couldn't love), a *proper* way of doing everything, even dying. And the proper way was strict, severe and inflexible. As boys there was a proper way to dress, which meant long-sleeved shirts, shorts, socks and shoes, and not a spot of dirt was to be seen on any of these at any time. In the tropical heat our uniform was like armour. There was a proper way of talking to your elders. Speak only when spoken to, and say sir and madam always. You were to show no pain; no tears were to be seen in public. Every minute of your life was an established routine, a habit predetermined not to offend God, society and Grandfather. Wealth had to be earned properly through dedicated hard work, honest business dealings and faith in the Almighty. Most important of all, we were not to reveal at any time our 'Samoan side' which, according to our grandmother, was 'uncivilized and pagan'.

I loved the strict, orderly world of my grandparents' household. In it I knew where I was, what I had to do, where I was going, and what everyone expected of me. My brothers struggled valiantly to survive within it. Later the always impish, clear-seeing Max described it as 'trying to shape yourself to fit into a rigid mould, like a demon trying to fit into a starched white Sunday suit'.

We started at St Andrews boarding school in 1934. I thrived in it because it was a replica of my grandparents' rigid world.

In 1936, Max graduated and, with our grandfather's proud approval, enlisted in the New Zealand Army; he fought and died in Italy in 1943. With enormous tears sliding down his face – it was the first and last time I would see him cry in public – my grandfather declared, during a memorial service at our church, that his beloved grandson 'had died a glorious death for God, King and Country'. (Our father wasn't invited to the service.)

Henry excelled at every major sport at our school but failed academically. Grandfather's reaction, when Henry returned home to work in the business, was an unforgiving silence. For three painful years Henry tried to be 'the glorified clerk' (his description) Grandfather wanted to turn him into, then he disappeared into the large silence of New Zealand's South Island. The silence ended, in June 1950, with a short note from one of Henry's friends informing us that Henry had died on Mt Cook in a mountain-climbing accident. In full view of his whole family, Grandfather tore the note into neat little pieces, rose slowly to his feet as if he was carrying Mt Cook on his now frail shoulders, and retreated into his study. The next morning, he emerged to tell us that 'in no way is *his* name to be mentioned in my presence!'

I excelled in my studies at high school and university, returning as a qualified accountant with a young wife, daughter of a successful Auckland lawyer, and whom my grandfather approved of whole-heartedly. Soon, after he was satisfied I was running our business efficiently, properly, Grandfather retired from 'active service' (his phrase). He died in 1961, a few months before Samoa became independent, something which he had dreaded and opposed because it meant 'the Samoans, the ignorant forces of anarchy, are going to run and ruin the country'.

He made me his sole heir.

That hot afternoon as I burned my father's treasure, large segments of that history paraded slowly through my mind. It was as if I was re-examining it and feeding it to the fire. My brothers kept returning, insisting on not allowing me to let the fire consume them; and the wonderful, magnificent imagery of our boyhood together eventually pushed all else from my heart.

With such beauty came the huge pain of loss, the unhealing wound that bled into an enormous rage when I realized that there could be no profit, no cure, to balance such a loss.

The evening hatched a consoling silence around me as I emptied the contents of the last boxes into the fire. I sat, dirty hands cupped to my cheeks, feeling as if the blood had been sucked out of my every cell.

The fire spluttered and began to die.

'Let's go home!' my son whispered.

Obediently I followed him to our pick-up. Handing me a clean rag and pointing at my face, he said, 'I've loaded all the books you saved on to the truck.'

I got into the truck, looked into the rear-view mirror, then wiped the tears and soot off my face.

I avoided looking at my son as he drove us home. Slowly I became aware that the smell (more stench than smell) of my father's mouldy, decaying treasure seemed to be smoking out of my pores. Once I brushed my hands through my hair, and they came away covered with soot which, in the thickening darkness, looked like blood.

'You didn't have to, Dad,' John said. It was the first time that day he had called me that, and I tried to clutch on to his forgiveness.

'It was mainly useless paper,' I said.

'You're lucky,' he said. 'You know a lot about him.'

I remained silent as our truck sped through the cicada-voiced evening up to Vailima.

As we got out of the truck in our garage, John said, 'I've saved three of the boxes. I didn't show them to you. One is for you; the other two are mine. I'll put yours in your study.' He was gone before I could protest.

For nearly a week the box sat in the armchair in my study. I avoided it. Finally, my wife sorted through it and informed me she had stored the books in my bookshelves and the folder in one of my desk drawers.

Last Thursday night I opened the folder for the first

time. In it is a letter from my father to my mother, and four drawings in coloured crayons: two by Max (as a seven-year-old), one by a six-year-old Henry, and one by me when I was five, all carefully labelled by our father.

My father's florid handwriting in blue ink is now barely visible in his letter to my mother.

As I started reading it, an itchy trembling began in my nose and, within seconds, it had emanated like rippling water throughout my body. I thumped the letter down on to the desk and clutched the desk edge with both hands tightly, until the shaking eased away like a receding tide, leaving me, once again, stranded on the jagged reef of my balloonfish migraine and my father's dismal confession of love for my mother.

Apia
14 June 1933

Dear Margaret,

I love you. I will always love you. I will give you a week. If you don't return with our children by the end of that time, I will consider our marriage ended. I won't even give your parents the satisfaction of contesting the custody of our children.

God bless you.

I shut the folder and hurried out on to the veranda overlooking the hills and sharp-edged ravines of Vailima. For a long time I gazed up into the ocean of stars. Around me, the night breathed heavily like a jealous lover.

I refused to look at the drawings that night. I retreated into our bedroom, stripped off my clothes, slid quietly into bed and, rolling into a ball against the warm stillness of my wife's side, tried to sleep.

. . . The cicada has stopped crying. The memory of its sound lingers in your head like the quivering wings of a monarch butterfly. You try to hold on to it but, in a brief while, it dissolves into a regretful whisper. You return to your desk. Finally you take the folder out of the drawer, pull out the four drawings and spread them out on your desk. On to the drawings drips the sweat from your arms. You use a piece of blotting paper to suck up the islands of sweat.

You scrutinize Max's first drawing. A scrawny yellow tree with four branches, like arms without hands, stands in the centre of the picture, under a strip of navy-blue sky. In the background is what looks like a line of snow-capped mountains with a red sun above it. In the right-hand corner of the picture is a tiny creature with a black, eyeless head and six orange legs extending from both sides of its body. To the left of the tree, halfway up the page, is a yellow bird with a huge black beak, one pink eye, and scarlet talons.

Across the bottom of the picture your father has printed: THIS IS BY MAX WHO IS SEVEN YEARS OLD. IT TELLS THE STORY OF A PARROT AND A MILLIPEDE WHO GO LOOKING FOR THE MOUNTAIN OF ICE. MAX TELLS ME THAT I AM THE THIN YELLOW TREE.

Max's second picture is in black and red. First you read what your father says about it at the bottom: THIS IS ABOUT A RED FISH IN THE BLACK SEA. You examine the picture from all different angles, trying to find the red fish. You can't. The picture remains a wild tangle of red and black lines, scribbles and whorls.

Henry's picture is an almost blank space inhabited, at the centre, by a round blue creature with two legs extending from its belly, and three toes on each foot. The creature is faceless. HENRY MY SIX YEAR OLD DREW THIS HANDSOME PORTRAIT OF ME, your father jokes at the bottom of the picture.

Your picture, the smallest of the four, is about six inches square. You are trapped utterly in that small space as you confront your five-year-old self. Curled into the prison of that space, like a frightened foetus, is a purple creature which is made up of six barely discernible circles joined together. Two antennae jut from the sides of the top circle, and two pairs of what you assume are legs curve out from the second and last circles. A thick yellow line, the sky, stretches across the top of the space. Right across the bottom edge, like the solid foundation of a house, your father says, THE ARMADILLO IS A MOST STRANGE CREATURE, SO MY FIVE YEAR OLD SON GABRIEL TELLS ME.

You break away from that space, with your father's song – and you admit it is a song – echoing throughout your depths like the bleep bleep bleeping of a satellite piercing the void, the black abyss, searching.

The dictionary is in your trembling hands. You search quickly. You find it:

armadillo (n) small burrowing animal of S. America with a body covered with a shell of bony plates, and the habit of rolling itself up into a ball when attacked.

Once again you find yourself out on the veranda, standing in the night, the cool wind blowing up the steep slopes, weaving and curling around your naked body, bringing with it the inconsolable grief of your parents and grandparents and brothers, your heritage, the profit and the loss no longer in equilibrium; your son, the avenger, is a victim of that terrible history, too.

So high the heavens glowing with a wondrous sheen. So high.

Even your migraine, your kind balloonfish, whose excruciating pain has saved you, always, has deserted you. You know it won't return, ever.

With that acceptance, you watch, fascinated, as your skin transforms itself slowly into a fabulous shell made up of bony plates, and in whose impregnable sanctuary your soul wants to roll up in a ball and die.

# Prospecting

It was mid-1893.

On his next trip into Apia with Barker, the papalagi trader and his closest friend, Mautu, the pastor of Satoa, brought home a new pick, a shovel and a bush-knife which he stored in the cupboard where he kept most of his valuable possessions. Curious about what he was going to use them for, Lalaga, his wife, and their four children waited for him to tell them that night during their usual English lesson. He didn't.

Next morning, which was Tuesday, they watched to see what he was going to do. After their meal at mid-morning, he put on a working lavalava, got out the new implements, and handed the shovel to Peleiupu, his thirteen-year-old daughter.

'May I come too?' Arona, his son, asked.

'Yes, may we?' chorused Ruta and Naomi, his youngest daughters. Mautu shook his head and started towards Barker's house which was situated across the malae under some breadfruit trees.

'You're too young!' Peleiupu remarked to the other children.

'So are you!' replied Ruta. Peleiupu flicked back her long mane, wheeled and followed Mautu, carrying the shovel like a rifle, across her shoulder.

She waited on the veranda, while Mautu went in to see Barker. Barker's three youngest children, snotty-nosed and naked, came out and, stopping a few paces away in a group, scrutinized her. Peleiupu knew them but, as yet, she refused to befriend any of Barker's children: she considered them too rude, too forward, altogether too papalagi, even though their mother was Samoan and they couldn't speak English.

'Is that a shovel?' the oldest, a girl of five, asked. Peleiupu nodded once.

'Is it *our* shovel?' the second girl asked, her right forefinger drilling into her right nostril. Peleiupu shook her head once.

'Shit!' exclaimed the youngest, a chubby male monster who was fingering his penis. Pretending she had been shocked by his remark, Peleiupu turned her back on them. 'Shit!' the boy repeated. His sisters giggled, then Peleiupu heard them running off the veranda and around the corner of the house. She tried not to laugh.

When Barker and Mautu came out, Barker was wearing his black, hobnailed boots. Around his waist was his cartridge belt. What he called his sun helmet was perched precariously on his huge mount of hair. Under his left arm was his canvas satchel in which, Peleiupu knew, he carried his pens, pencils and paper. His sleek rifle was in his right hand. The great adventurer that Mautu had told them about, thought Peleiupu.

'Where are we going?' she asked Mautu. He motioned with his head towards the plantations.

'It might rain,' Barker remarked in English, gazing briefly up at the dark blue clouds covering the top of the range.

Shaking his head, Mautu said, in English, 'No, it not rain. It is fine weather.'

Peleiupu's heart skipped with joy: she understood most of what they had said. Not just words any more; now sentences as well. (Barker was teaching her father English, and he, in turn, was teaching her and her brother and sisters.)

'Hurry! Hurry!' Barker called in Samoan to his aiga in

the fale behind the house. Two of his wife's brothers, Moamoa and Tuvanu, came running carrying another pick, bush-knives, and what Peleiupu thought were frying-pans without handles. 'Where the food?' Barker asked them abruptly in Samoan. Both men were middle-aged and had children. Moamoa scurried back to the fale. 'Fool! Fool!' Barker called after him. 'You can't trust these people!' Barker said in English to Mautu.

When Moamoa was back with the basket of food they started off, with Barker and Mautu leading, setting a stiff marching pace. Peleiupu almost had to run to keep up.

People in the fale they passed greeted them with invitations to stop and eat. Their group stopped briefly every time, and Mautu refused their invitations politely. A dog, fur all a-bristling, rushed at them with ferocious barks and snapping fangs. 'Alu! Alu!' Barker barked back at it. The poor creature cringed away, its tail between its legs.

Alongside the track, that was islanded with puddles, the vegetation was still sparkling with dew, and soon their clothes were wet from it. Peleiupu felt strong, invigorated, alive with anticipation, the adventure unravelling, and merrily smashed her reflection in the puddles with her feet. As they passed through the dark-green crops, trees, creepers and shrubs, she imagined they were swimming through a soundless sea world, where everything was lush green, led by the courageous Captain Barker, son of the English Earl, and his loyal native lieutenant Mautu.

Suddenly, into her day-dreaming, Barker's voice said, 'Gold,' and she glanced up at Barker's back, hoping to understand more, but Barker was speaking too fast.

They veered off the main track and crossed over creeper-covered ground through a plantation of bananas to the Satoa River.

On the edge of the bank they stood and surveyed the

river and the valley that meandered, like a gigantic centipede, up through foothills to the centre range. The river was faintly brown with silt as it rippled leisurely through narrow strips of boulders, rocks and pebbles sparkling in the sun. The light breeze brought with it, from the mountains, the odour of dark, decaying vegetation.

While they watched him, Barker found a large tree-trunk nearby, brushed the creepers off it, sat down, opened his satchel, took out a board, spread out sheets of blank paper on it, then, pencil poised in his right hand, he studied the terrain before them for a long, hushed while. Quietly, Peleiupu edged over and stood looking down, over his shoulder, at the paper. Mautu stabbed his bush-knife into the soil at his feet and, dangling his legs over the river bank, sat gazing at the water. Into the cool shade of a clump of bananas, Moamoa and Tuvanu retreated, and from there observed what Barker was doing. Already waves of heat were brimming visibly up from the beds of boulders and stones below.

When the hand clutching the pencil moved, it was like a quick spider drawing with all its legs. Soon black lines, a whole network of them, covered the paper. Peleiupu recognized it as a map of the river valley and the area around it. She had once seen a sketch map in one of Mautu's books.

Barker held it up to Mautu who came over and, studying it, said in English, 'Good, good!' Just like Barker would have said.

'I think we should start here.' Barker pointed with his pencil at the area of sand and pebbles on his map, then down at it in the valley. 'Then here on our next visit.' The next area was a few hundred yards up-river.

Just before they made their way down into the shallow valley, Barker shook Mautu's hand and, smiling, said, 'Good luck!' Peleiupu was even more puzzled than before.

The river was shallow where they were, beds of stones protruded from the water at midstream. Mautu took one of the shallow pans and squatted in the water. Stabbing the shovel into the pulpy sand, Barker pushed down on it with his booted foot until the shovel head was buried and then, wrenching up a shovelful of sand, tipped it into Mautu's pan. Fascinated, Peleiupu, Moamoa and Tuvanu watched.

'I not know how,' Mautu said in English to Barker.

'Let me.' Barker took the panful of pebbly sand, lowered it into the water and moved it back and forth, washing out the sand until only the bits of rock and pebbles were left. He then picked out the bits with his fingers and examined them. 'Nothing yet,' he said to Mautu. 'Take the other pan.' Mautu did so. Barker, in his broken Samoan, instructed Moamoa and Tuvanu to fill the pans with the sandy material whenever he told them to do so.

Peleiupu crouched in the water in her father's shadow and observed every move he was making. Mautu's eyes were alive with a brightness she hadn't seen there before. The water was cool around her feet and ankles; periodically she scooped up handfuls of it and washed her face with it.

Relentlessly the sun pressed down. Neither Mautu nor Barker noticed it and, whenever Moamoa and Tuvanu were slow, Barker hurled orders at them. Even in her father's shadow Peleiupu found the heat becoming painful, so she lay down in the water, with only her face and head above it. The cool water tingled on her body.

They shifted up-river along the water's edge whenever Barker decided nothing was to be found at a particular spot.

At noon, Peleiupu whispered to Mautu that she was hungry. Mautu told her and the other two men to go into the shade and have some food.

From the healing shade of trees, Peleiupu munched her food and watched them digging up the sand and sifting it in their pans, oblivious to the heat shimmering around them in visible waves like hungry swarms of mosquitoes. They seemed locked in a time they never wanted to leave.

Mautu was the first to break from the spell and hurry into the shade. He ate quickly, all the time watching Barker, finished and scrambled out again.

'Lazy! Lazy!' Barker shouted over to Moamoa and Tuvanu who got up reluctantly, cursing under their breath, and went out.

'Gold,' Peleiupu remembered Barker saying earlier that morning, as she watched. She fell asleep and dreamt of Mautu looming above her, his chest puffed out, his face beaming with a golden light, then, digging his hands into the centre of his chest, he prized open his rib-cage and out of the cavern of his chest gushed a river of liquid gold in which she splashed and laughed and laughed.

They got home that evening as Lalaga was lighting the lamp and, without speaking to their inquisitive aiga, got some soap and towels and went and bathed in the communal pool beside the church. Their whole aiga were in the main fale ready for the lotu when they returned. Mautu put on a shirt. Peleiupu brought him the Bible.

Straight after their meal, during which Mautu ate as if he was caught utterly in his own thoughts, Mautu went to where he usually slept, drew the curtain behind him, and they soon heard him snoring.

Peleiupu, anticipating her mother, gave her a vivid, matter-of-fact description of what she called 'their expedition' but omitted her speculation that Barker and Mautu were prospecting for gold.

'What can they be looking for?' Lalaga asked, more to herself than Peleiupu who shrugged her shoulders. Lalaga left.

When her brother and sisters and the other young people in their aiga gathered eagerly around her,

Peleiupu re-told her story, this time with extravagant embellishments, dramatic flourishes, hilariously accurate imitations of Barker's Samoan, and deliberately misleading guesses as to what the two men were searching for. One, perhaps they were mapping the course of the Satoa River. Two, perhaps because both men were scientific, they were just working out the types of sand, rocks, mud and pebbles found in the valley. Three, perhaps they were excavating for the sites of ancient villages, hoping to find priceless artefacts. Four, perhaps – and this was the remotest possibility of all – they were acting out an adventure they had read in one of Barker's books.

Tired from the expedition, she tumbled into a deep sleep soon after telling her tale.

The other children lay awake late into the night envying her and speculating among themselves, in whispers, concerning what Barker and Mautu were up to.

By the morning meal, everyone in Satoa was talking about the expedition. At this point, with everyone hungrily awaiting the unravelling of the mystery, no one advanced the possibility that perhaps both men had gone mad or were chasing mirages as described in the Holy Book, the very thing that Peleiupu was protecting her father against by not mentioning gold.

For Peleiupu, two impatient days had to be tolerated before their next 'expedition up-river' (a phrase she had read in a book). During that time, Mautu spent the afternoons with Barker going over the sketch map and marking in large red Xs their next diggings. For the first time, Mautu told her to stay home and help Lalaga. Hurt by this, she was a sullen, easily angered, resentful helper, and she had frequent quarrels with the other children and especially Arona who, as the only son, resented her for being a favoured companion to their father. Arduous up-river expeditions were for boys, not girls, he complained to Lalaga who, when alone in bed with a silent Mautu that night, explained that it was time he took his *only* son with him and not Peleiupu. 'We shall see,' he said absent-mindedly and was immediately lost in his thoughts again.

'Your children, apart from Peleiupu, do not exist for you!' she complained.

'What did you say?'

She slapped the mats she was lying on and, trying to keep her voice down, said, 'Never mind!'

'You are angry with me?' he asked gently.

'No!' she snapped. Then quietly she asked, 'What is happening to you? What are you searching for? You speculate, you dream, you pursue figments of Barker's imagination and what you read in those books!'

'I pursue God's mystery. His depth. His secrets. I want to understand Him.' It was stated simply with total belief.

'It can lead you to heresy. Have you thought of that?'

'How can it be, when I know that God is Everything, including the wonders and dreams and fantasies and visions of the Imagination and Mind?' With that she was lost, she could not grasp his meaning.

'And this – this unreal search for gold?'

'Did Peleiupu tell you that?'

'No, your clever, loyal daughter tried to put me off your track.'

'But what is so unreal about it? No one has tried to see if there is gold here, have they?'

Caught again by his logic, she felt like shouting. 'But everyone says there is no gold here!'

'But where is the actual proof?' When she didn't reply, he caressed her shoulder and said, 'I love you and our children more than my own life.'

'Soon you will be lost from my understanding,' she said, almost in tears. 'Please stop this search for gold before our people think you've gone . . .' She couldn't say it.

'Yes?' he asked. She refused to say it.

While it was still dark on Friday morning, with a chilly wind weaving in from the sea, he woke Peleiupu and Arona, and they dressed without waking the others, and, carrying a basket of food and their implements, went to Barker's house. The dew-covered grass prickled under their feet.

Barker and a yawning Moamoa and a half-asleep Tuvanu were waiting on the veranda. Without talking they were soon into the solemn shadows and the breathing silence of the plantations.

That day, the sun pursued them again. They covered about half a mile of river bank, stopping, digging, sifting panfuls of sandy material, then shifting further inland. Barker and Mautu, oblivious to everything else, confined their talking to intermittent instructions to Moamoa and Tuvanu; the two children were like their shadows, always beside them, saying nothing, watching.

At mid-morning, Peleiupu noticed that the still air immediately around them was tainted with Barker's flying-fox smell which worsened as he sweated and as they moved into the humid dampness of the bush which, at the start of the foothills, groped right down to the water's edge.

They found nothing that day.

At the to'ona'i at his home on Sunday, some of the village elders questioned Mautu politely, obliquely, about his search. Light-heartedly he told them that they had found nothing yet. No one asked him what they were looking for: they had heard rumours, started by Moamoa and Tuvanu, that precious metals were being prospected for.

Lalaga refused to ask him about it, while Peleiupu, now the veteran explorer, let Arona explain to the other children what had happened so far. The slow Arona stuck, in his story, to the bare facts and details.

The following week, they went out three times.

Moamoa and Tuvanu, tired from the work and Barker's abuse, didn't appear the last time, a Friday, so the still-eager Peleiupu and Arona carried the implements and food.

After a heavy night's rain, the ground under the bush at the river's edge was soft and stank of decay; their feet sank into it up to the ankles. The undergrowth was denser, more tangled, and they had to cut a track through it. Around them the sad air was a blue sea of steam through which swam rapacious swarms of mosquitoes, which Peleiupu and Arona fought off with small leafy branches. The river banks shot up sharply into rugged escarpments, hills and ridges, all smothered with virgin bush, which made them feel they were being watched.

As they worked there was little conversation. There was only the rushing sound of the now swiftly flowing water and the occasional lost cries of birds. Around them Peleiupu sensed the bush world growing, growing.

Late in the afternoon, wet and tired, the skins on their hands and faces wrinkled with the cold, they retreated from the bush and headed for home, locked into themselves, and Peleiupu wondered if her father and Barker were going to give up.

That weekend, the Satoans, encouraged by Moamoa's and Tuvanu's funny comments about the expedition, started joking about it behind Mautu's back. The young people in Satoa, however, maintained their faith in the search.

On Monday morning, with the barely visible drizzle whirling around them as they tramped up the valley, Peleiupu sensed a more dogged determination in the two men.

The bush still steamed with an inescapable darkness, and, as they entered it, it closed around them. Little light. They worked.

They went twice more that week. Still nothing. The

drizzle continued. The terrain became more rugged, wilder, more difficult to penetrate. The mosquitoes fought for their blood.

Another week, then Arona's shovel stabbed, a few inches into the water-logged ground, and struck a solid but hollow object. He pressed down on the shovel with his large foot. The shovel refused to sink down any further. He scraped the mud off the object. Through the weeping scar in the mud, an opaque whiteness shone. He scraped off more mud.

'What is it?' Peleiupu asked.

'Don't know,' he replied.

Their father looked down. He took Arona's shovel and dug around the object. Suddenly, he stopped.

'What is it?' asked Peleiupu. Mautu started covering the object with soil again but Barker reached over, grasped the shovel handle, and stopped him.

With his boot, Barker pushed the mud aside, reached down into the shallow hole with both hands, grasped the object, and pulled it up. The children cringed back. It was a human skull. In the blue light, it looked so nakedly white. It was veined with black mud.

With his hands, Barker brushed all the dirt off it. 'Wonder how it got here?' he asked, poking his fingers into the eye sockets.

'We go now!' Mautu said to him in English. The children gathered the implements quickly.

Barker, without saying anything, started digging up the ground around where the skull had lain. Peleiupu could feel her father's mounting anger as he stood there watching Barker. Bit by bit, as Barker dug, the broken human skeleton was revealed.

Panting heavily from the exertion, Barker asked, 'It's so far inland, how did it get here?'

Mautu refused to answer. 'Let's go home,' he instructed his children.

'But it's early!' insisted Barker. 'There's nothing to be afraid of either.'

83

'The message, it is clear,' Mautu said in English. 'There is nothing here. Not now!'

'But the mystery, don't you sense the mystery? How come *he* is here. There may be others as well!'

'We leave it alone!' Mautu said. It was an order.

For a moment Barker hesitated, then, dismissing Mautu with a curt nod, started exploring the nearby ground, with decisive stabs of his shovel.

Mautu wheeled and started for home. His children followed him.

Behind them, caught in the blue tangle of bush, they could hear Barker foraging like a hungry boar. Even when, miles later, they were free of the bush, they could see Barker in their minds, black with wet and sweat, his muscular body pulsating with inquisitive blood, his eyes focused hypnotically on the ground, his arms pounding the shovel into the softness, searching for the bones, the skeletons.

At home, they didn't tell anyone about their terrible find.

After their evening meal, during which Mautu ate little, Mautu disappeared into the wet darkness.

'Barker won't find any more, will he?' Arona whispered to Peleiupu when they were trying to sleep.

'No,' she reassured him. Around them the dark was filled with aitu and other fearful phantoms.

'I'm – I'm scared!' he murmured.

'Mautu will make sure it's all right!' she said. He shifted closer to her. 'Go to sleep now,' she whispered.

They woke early but Mautu had left already. They ran to Barker's house; he was gone too.

It drizzled again all day. Everything smelled of mould and dampness. Even the sun refused to leave its bed of black cloud. While Peleiupu and Arona worked around their home and, in the afternoon, attended their mother's classes, they waited anxiously for Mautu to appear out of the rain.

Miserably wet and grim-faced, he came, bathed,

conducted the lotu, ate quickly, and then disappeared into his side of the fale behind the curtain. Peleiupu went to ask if they were having an English lesson that night. She peeped through the gap in the curtain. He was sitting cross-legged, arms folded across his chest, eyes shut firmly, praying silently. In the gloom, she saw the bright aura of almost overpowering sadness surrounding him like a second skin.

Lalaga called her and Arona, when the other children were in their mosquito nets.

'What happened yesterday?' she asked them.

'Nothing,' replied Peleiupu, gazing straight into her mother's face.

'Arona?' Lalaga demanded. Arona, who had been sitting with bowed head, glanced up at Peleiupu. 'Arona?' repeated Lalaga. Arona bowed his head again and picked at the edge of the mat he was sitting on. 'Your father is in pain. I must know why!'

'Perhaps it was something that happened today,' Peleiupu offered.

'I am waiting!' Lalaga said. 'Arona, do you love your father?' Arona nodded almost imperceptibly. 'Then you must tell me.'

Arona looked at Peleiupu. She nodded once, finally.

'A skull,' he said, without looking at Lalaga.

'We found a skull and his bones,' said Peleiupu.

'Where?'

'Way up-river. Arona found it with his shovel. Barker dug it up. Then the rest of the skeleton,' said Peleiupu.

'Mautu did not want Barker to dig it up,' Arona continued slowly.

'Mautu was angry when Barker refused to stop, and he brought us back. Barker continued to dig for more bones.'

'You must not tell anyone else about it,' she instructed them. They nodded. She reached over and caressed Arona's shoulder. 'There is no need to be afraid.'

Later when Lalaga went to bed she knew that Mautu

was only pretending to be asleep but she decided not to question him. She lay down beside him.

In her dreams, she heard his desperate cry for help. Waking, she found him sitting beside her in the darkness. His muted weeping was an incessant low stirring into which she reached, found his face, and held it between her warm hands. His tears washed over the backs of her fingers.

'They are here all around me,' he murmured. 'They filled my sleep with their cries, their disquiet, their awful dying!' He paused and, when she took her hands away, he wiped his face with a corner of his sleeping-sheet. 'We searched for gold and found *them*!'

'So there is more than one?' she asked.

'Yes. We spent all day yesterday clearing the ground and finding them clinging even to the roots of the trees, as if they hadn't wanted to die!'

'An old burial place?'

'If only it was that, I would be less disturbed. They were all killed, slaughtered!'

'What are you going to do?' She was satisfied that his gruesome discovery had shocked him back to the realities she knew, and she hoped he would remain there.

'There are more to be dug up. Once we have done that, we will bring them down and give them a Christian burial.'

'We must tell our village and they will help you.'

'Not yet,' he said. 'When we discover all of them, I will tell Satoa and we will all go up and bring them down and bury them beside the church.'

'How did they die?'

'Barker says it was a battle.'

'Up at the top of the nearest hill under the vegetation we have found the remnants of an ancient village. Barker thinks the village was invaded, conquered, burnt to the ground, and most of its inhabitants killed and left there.'

'But is there a story of that in Satoan history?'

'Not that I know of. It must have happened a long time ago and been quickly forgotten. Or that unfortunate village was destroyed even before Satoa was founded.'

At dawn, when Peleiupu and Arona got up to go with Mautu, Lalaga told them not to. They obeyed her when they saw the weight of pain in their father.

Every day for a week, Barker and Mautu went up into the hills. Mautu's hair was suddenly freckled with grey, his physical fragility became more pronounced, his conversations were no longer laced with *that* spark, he moved like a creature caught in a self-destructive dream. Conscious of the sadness they saw each day in their pastor, the Satoans stopped joking about *the* expedition. Their pastor (misled by that insane papalagi) in his incredible search for gold had discovered a new pain, and they were waiting for him to reveal it to them.

The following week, Barker and Mautu went up twice. The second time, on a Thursday, Mautu insisted with Lalaga that Peleiupu and Arona accompany him.

'But why?' she asked.

'Arona found the first person. Peleiupu was there too. Now they must come and see the rest of them before we bring them down.'

'I still don't understand!' she insisted. 'Our children are still too young to be near – near *those* things!'

'They must learn what death is; they must see *the people*. They will not frighten them.'

Again, she couldn't comprehend him.

The area where they had found the first skeleton was now a fairly large clearing, basking in bright sunlight. All the undergrowth had been cleared away; some of the trees had been cut down, chopped into short pieces, and stacked by the water. In the clearing, among the boulders, was a scatter of shallow graves, about sixty in all. In them, lying in grotesque postures, were the glittering skeletons. Many of them were badly broken, shattered, scattered; many skulls and bones were missing; some of the graves were occupied by more than one skeleton.

'Don't be frightened,' Mautu encouraged Peleiupu and Arona. 'After being with them for this length of time, I *know* they won't harm us.' He walked round the graves. 'Come and see them.'

Barker, who was standing back, called in Samoan, 'Go, they only harmless bones!' Peleiupu saw her father wince at Barker's remark. 'I not know why your father tell me help him dig up all that useless bones!' Barker looked away hurriedly when Mautu glared at him, sat down on a log, and started scraping the mud off his boots.

'Come on,' Mautu invited his children. Arona moved protectively against Peleiupu as they walked into the midst of *the people*. 'It's all right!' she whispered, trying to control her own trembling. They both refused to look down at the skeletons, feeling as if they were at a great height and would tumble to their deaths if they looked down.

'Look, no harm!' Mautu called, holding up one of the skulls.

Gold, Peleiupu heard Barker repeat in her head. Gold. Gold. Gold. Gold. She gazed down and the heap of bones in the grave in front of her looked golden in the sunlight. All around a golden luminosity was bursting up from the mouths of the graves, and inside her the bones transformed themselves into huge pua blossoms, and she was floating through a garden of white magic flowers.

She broke from her delicious wandering when Arona said, 'Mautu is right. They will not harm us.'

'No, they are our friends,' she said.

After their inspection, Mautu motioned to them to follow him. A narrow track, which Barker and Mautu had cut, led uphill from the clearing and disappeared into the bush.

The slope was steep and slippery and they had to hold on to nearby branches as they clambered up the hill. Disturbed by their noise, gnats, butterflies and other insects fluttered up from the undergrowth.

The top of the hill was covered by huge trees matted together at their heads by creepers and lianas which allowed little light to penetrate to the ground.

'This is where they lived,' Mautu said, pointing at the creeper-covered mounds that lay under the trees and spread out ahead into the vegetation. 'Those were the paepae of their fale. That is all that is left. It was a fairly large village.'

'But why did they live up here?' asked Peleiupu.

'It was always safer to build your village in a well-protected place. Up here the people could see who was coming. They built a palisade around their village. The river was their source of water.'

'What was it called?' she asked.

'I don't know. Perhaps an old person in Satoa can tell us.' Their voices sounded unreal in the enclosed vegetation. 'Are you still frightened?' Mautu asked Arona who shook his head and smiled. 'You will remember them and their village for the rest of your lives, carrying them as part of your dead, in your blood.'

Right then, Barker broke noisily through the undergrowth, and, confronting Mautu, his face red with exertion and sweat pouring off him, said, in English, 'And what, my pastor friend, are you going to do with our mountain of bones and skulls?'

'You never going to understand, eh?' Mautu asked sadly in English.

'No, he not understand!' Peleiupu heard herself say in English. Surprised, she glanced up at Mautu, then at Barker, who were both gazing in amazement at her because it was the *first* time she had ever spoken English to them.

'Graveyards and dead villages produce wonderful surprises!' Barker laughed.

'Yes, the Dead can open the minds of innocent children to wisdom,' Mautu said in Samoan and with pride.

Later as they made their way down, Arona asked Peleiupu what she had said in English. That Barker would never understand, she replied.

'Understand what?' he asked.

'What Mautu told us about the Dead and how important they are.'

'I didn't understand Mautu either,' Arona sighed. 'I'm too young!'

'Someday you too will understand,' she consoled him but immediately experienced a twinge of guilt for deliberately lying to him that she had understood.

'I want . . . I want so much!' he exclaimed.

'So much what?'

'Everything! To know everything!'

'But no one can do that!'

'Someday I will!' His determination made her experience a more abundant love for him. 'I want to be grown-up, *now*!'

By the river, as they wandered once again among the graves, they experienced no fear, as though they had left it up on the hill in the village snared in the choking tentacles of the bush. Arona even stopped at one of the graves, sat at the edge and dangled his feet until they were only a few inches above the skull. His feet looked like large fish-hooks seeking the mouth of the skull. Peleiupu sat down beside him and remembered how the graves, the bones, had burst with a golden light.

That Friday and Saturday the young men of Mautu's school dug a series of graves beside the church. Most of the men of Satoa, when they heard about it, joined the work. At the Sunday morning service, Mautu described, from the pulpit, his expedition and what he and Barker had discovered. He asked that their village give 'the people' (his phrase) a Christian burial. The church buzzed with questions. During to'onai, Mautu answered all the elders' questions. None of them knew anything about the village on the hill.

Sao, the tu'ua of Satoa, called a meeting of the matai at his fale on Monday morning; and after a weighty discussion concerning the burying of so many strangers in their village, they organized a party to go up to the hills, with Mautu on Tuesday, and bring down 'the people'.

The large party was led by Sao and Mautu who wore ties and their white Sunday suits. All the other elders and their wives were in their Sunday wear too. The untitled men, who were to carry 'the people', wore only black lavalava. No children were allowed to go.

They reached the graves just before midday. Immediately, Mautu conducted a service. A hymn was sung; he read from the Bible; then prayed. Standing at the perimeter of the clearing in their best clothes and caught in the bright stillness of the hills and mountains, they seemed incongruous, strangers visiting another village for the first time.

After Mautu's prayer, the old men moved into the shade, while the women worked in groups oiling the bones with coconut oil and wrapping them up in tapa cloth, as was the custom. No one spoke. No one was afraid.

When all 'the people' were clothed, as it were, in tapa, the young men picked them up and, carrying them on their shoulders, followed Mautu and the elders down towards Satoa. Beside them the river rippled and swerved and danced and fingered its way towards the sea.

Awaiting them around the graves beside the church were the rest of Satoa.

Again no one spoke. A hush lay over the village.

The young men lined 'the people', eighty bundles, in a row below the church steps. Gradually, like a rising tide, the old women started the customary funeral wailing, and their sound was that of the mourning sea. Many of the people wept. Peleiupu and Arona, who were standing beside Lalaga, cried silently.

His white suit shimmering in the afternoon sun, Mautu stood on the church steps. 'Let us sing Hymn 134: "God be with us now in our Sorrow".' The powerful singing broke up to the crystal-clear sky and sent the heat retreating into the shade.

'Lord, we gather here today to send to you people we never knew!' prayed Mautu, and, as he prayed, Peleiupu saw thin lines of tears trickling down his cheeks, and she wept some more.

Another hymn, then Mautu's sermon. 'The Dignity of Satoa, from the youngest to the most noble, we are gathered here today to mourn the death of brothers and sisters who died before Christ's Message reached our shores. We never knew them but up in the wilderness they have been waiting for us to come and find them with love, to rescue them from the Darkness in which they were dwelling, to save their wandering souls and send them peacefully to God . . .' His meaning was a steady healing feeling that cooled them in the heat. Once again he was *their* pastor with the spark, the fire, to make them believe, and who, in his foolish but God-determined search for gold, had lost the fire until he had discovered 'the people' who brought him back to them. And many more of them wept.'. . . In one of the kingdoms of South America there lives to this day a creature called the Webbed-light. It has no body and yet it can become anything it wants. It lives in the air above the highest peak of the Andes and watches over all the creatures in the Kingdom. Every year, before the season of Death, usually associated with Winter when ice and snow kill everything, this wonderful Creature pierces its own throat and, assuming the shape of the eagle, flies over the barren land and, crying the cry of a new-born lamb, its rich blood gushes from the wound in its throat and on entering the soil makes it strong enough to endure the winter and, in spring, burst forth again with new life.

'This creature, people of Satoa, is like our God who, with His blood, saves us every year, every minute of our lives, so that we can save others in their winter. Today, we are saving, for our God, the souls of our sisters and brothers who have endured a winter in the wilderness. They died a pagan death in the Days of Darkness. Today, we convert their souls to Christianity. Today, we mourn their death and, at the same time, celebrate their waking to God's brilliant Light and Love . . .' He went on to soothe their sorrow.

In groups, the men took 'the people' and lowered them gently into their graves. Then Mautu said, 'Dust to dust, earth to earth', and they scattered the rich grains of earth over 'the people'.

They sang hymns while the men filled the graves.

After everyone else had gone home, Peleiupu and Arona and Ruta and Naomi and a small group of their friends lingered in the shade of the pua trees beside the graves.

'They were killed, weren't they?' Ruta asked Arona who, in turn, looked at Peleiupu, who nodded.

'In a war?' Naomi asked. Peleiupu nodded again. The mounds of earth were drying quickly in the heat.

'Their aitu will haunt our village!' Naomi remarked.

'No,' said Peleiupu. 'Because we have saved them, they will not harm us.'

'Are you sure?' Ruta asked.

'I *am* sure!' Peleiupu said, turning to go.

As they followed Peleiupu, Arona said, 'Barker didn't come?'

'No, he didn't come,' replied Peleiupu.

'Why not?' asked Naomi.

'You ask too many questions!' she said.

'Yes, she's always asking about this and that and this and that!' said Ruta.

'So are you!' Naomi accused her. Immediately an

argument erupted between them. Peleiupu ran off; Arona followed her; their friends dispersed too, leaving Naomi and Ruta to the twitching heat and sun.

From their fale the next day, at mid-morning, they observed Barker and his wife and children and their aiga arriving at the graveyard, with shovels and picks and baskets of river stones and pebbles. They started piling the stones and pebbles onto the graves, neatly. Mautu went out to them.

'So you not believe in our bones, eh?' Mautu asked Barker in English.

'I never said that!' Barker replied. Mautu chuckled. 'I suppose being human like us they needed to be buried decently.' Paused, then turning and focusing his smile on Mautu, said, 'And, after all, we found them and are therefore *equally* responsible for them. You can say we *are* now their family!' They laughed together for a long while, and the others were puzzled by it. 'You can even say we struck gold!' And their laughter continued to echo around the graves and ripple through the church and dance out across the malae and dive mischievously into every Satoa home, and brought all the Satoans running, skipping, hobbling, scuttling to the graves of their people.

And while the old people and Mautu and Barker sat joking in the shade, everyone else built up the graves with the sleek, black stones and pebbles that the young people brought in baskets from the river.

Mautu's aiga and other nearby aiga made umu and cooked a delicious variety of food, and, when the work on the graves was finished, they invited everyone into Mautu's home and they ate heartily and laughed uproariously at Barker's and Mautu's exaggerated stories about their futile, mad, ridiculous prospecting for gold up-river, up-valley.

It was the first time Barker had been in Mautu's home. As the sun was setting, after Barker and all the

Satoans had left with their infectious laughter, Peleiupu cut some branches from the pua trees and started planting them between the graves. Arona observed her for a while, then dug up some shrubs and flowers from around their fale, took them and, without saying anything to Peleiupu, replanted them around the central grave. Ruta and Naomi and a frisky gaggle of friends got more plants from the neighbouring area and planted them around some of the other graves. Yet more children came with more flowers, shrubs and plants.

And the same darkness that fell on the deserted village on the hill in the wilderness fell protectively over a noisy, mushrooming garden of children.

# I Will be Our Saviour
# from the Bad Smell

On Wednesday morning, we woke in our humble village, Saula, to find ourselves caught nauseatingly in the grasp of what we would later call the Bad Smell. Immediately, I approximated it to the stench of a coral reef that is dying above water level, but after rushing to the beach and scrutinizing the reef, I knew it wasn't — the reef was aswirl with fierce waves.

Slowly I strolled back to our main house trying to identify the ingredients of the evil concoction that was the Bad Smell: rotten fruit, decaying flesh, rancid cheese (I've never tasted that), brackish water and swamp mud, the list was limitless. All around me, I could see that our people were excitedly discussing the evil invader in their houses and fale while preparing their morning meal.

I didn't want to alarm my aiga unnecessarily, so when I entered our house, and my children, hands grasped firmly to their noses, attacked me with their shrill questions, I pretended it wasn't *that* bad by saying, 'It won't last, it'll go away, just a dead little something somewhere!'

Meleane, my mother, who was helping the children get dressed for school, said, 'It is like death!'

'The children are listening!' I cautioned her. She got the message immediately.

'Well, it is like decaying breadfruit!' Less alarming.

I nodded and smiled, noticing that my wife, our children and our other numerous relatives were now unclenching their fingers from their noses. (We all prefer dead fruit to dead people!)

Soon we were all gathered in our back fale for our morning meal.

'It must be coming in from the sea,' my wife theorized. (My wife thinks a lot and expresses her views, opinions and prejudices openly and often.)

'Maybe,' I murmured, still pretending the Bad Smell was a harmless nothing.

'She is correct,' my mother agreed with my wife. (My mother, now in her insecure seventies and not blessed with white-haired wisdom, is very cautious and rarely offers any views whether commonplace or controversial.) And with that affirmation, I watched my whole aiga – there were about twenty people in the fale – turn their noses seawards and take long sniffs, trying to confirm my wife's claim. The sea was a slowly shifting mass of dull silver glimpsed through the tangle of palms and fau on the shore.

'Don't think it's the sea!' my brother Siaki, the always provocative but useless dissenter, attacked everyone who then looked at him. 'It can't be the sea!' Siaki, as usual, was sitting at the back of the fale beside the young people who were serving our meal; he is never far from any food source, and he looks it, being what my wife has described as 'a solid tune of fat'. 'Must be a dead animal somewhere,' Siaki added. Siaki, though older than me, had not been given our aiga's highest matai title (that was conferred on me) because according to our mother, who still spoils him, 'he is too delicate and weak to assume the heavy responsibilities of a matai'. He is fifty-five years old and, as far as I am aware, has never been sick (seriously) in all those years.

'The smell of one dead animal can't fill the whole air of our village!' I insisted, knowing Siaki wasn't going to contradict me – he rarely does, because he owes his comfortable life to me. Siaki started to sulk immediately.

'And it isn't the smell of a dead animal.' My wife whipped Siaki a bit more. Siaki opened his mouth to speak. 'It *can't* be the smell of a dead animal!' She closed his mouth.

Because we, the elders of our aiga, were disagreeing about the source of the Bad Smell, the others were now visibly confused: some had their noses fixed on the sea, others on the malae, and others on the sky.

'What is it then?' My mother tried to rescue Siaki, her favourite.

Excrement! the word ballooned in my mind like a pink bubble, but I wasn't going to release the bubble publicly and before our innocent children. No one else was going to either, though I sensed that at least half of them were thinking the same thing. It isn't moral or aristocratic to mention excrement (in any form) in public, even though TAE (shit) is the first word most children learn to utter.

'Could be the smell of trees drying in the bush,' I side-tracked them.

'Yes, could be.' My wife took our aiga's thoughts farther away from excrement. Most of us now focused our silent sniffing on the plantations, the bush and hills.

'Bring our food now,' my mother instructed. The young people served us, the elders, with fa'alifu and mugs of hot cocoa.

While we ate, we tried not to inhale the Bad Smell. But it attacked us relentlessly, as if It now filled every crevice and space in Saula.

Our village, as I have said, is small. We have only about thirty matai, and we meet as a council, a fono, at our tu'ua's main fale, every Thursday morning starting at 10 a.m.

We met the day after the Bad Smell had arrived. For

a frantic while we tried discussing village affairs, such as repairing our school and inspecting our plantations, but the Bad Smell's omnipotent presence became our only topic of discussion.

Our tu'ua, the venerable Pesemalie, who is about eighty and married to my father's sister and the wisest human being I know, opened the heated discussion with the question, 'This Bad Smell, where is It coming from?' (His polite name for the stench, in time, became *our* name for the invisible insidious invader.)

Each matai in turn explained his theory about the Bad Smell using long, ornate and elaborate speeches. (Need, so a papalagi proverb goes, is the mother of invention and poetry!)

Those among us whose tempers are short-fused like dynamite found ourselves raving frenziedly about the Bad Smell. For instance, Moefalo Ioane, a good friend but an impatient man who always acts before he thinks, declared: 'It is the Devil who has sent this curse. We have to locate Its source and burn It, exorcize It . . .' His whole face and body inflated visibly with an angry frustration. '. . . My wife and aiga can't stand it any more. We must act, drive the Devil away! We must slay It!'

After the speeches, Pesemalie summed up our views thus, 'We all agree that we must find the evil source of the Bad Smell and kill It. We will appoint a committee to explore the land, sea and air . . .'

A committee of four was duly appointed and Pesemalie, my wise mentor, appointed me committee chairman. I was the only matai who had undergone a good science education at the district high school, and I was fluent in English, Pesemalie justified my important appointment.

'You are to lead the army that is to save our village from Evil!' Pesemalie exhorted our committee. Full almost to bursting with pride, I began to understand for the first time why I had felt, throughout my life, that

I had been born for a special mission and that one lucid day that mission would be revealed to me.

After our council meeting, our committee of four assembled in the sitting room of my house.

Tila, the oldest, is blind in his left eye (a cricket-game accident in his boyhood); his skin is splotched with enormous continents of tinea; a little formal education, acquired at pastor's school, inhabits his head. He usually talks fluently and poetically but mostly about nothing. His powers of oratory were, I surmised, his main qualification for our investigating committee.

Our second investigator was Fa'afofoga, a middle-aged fisherman who says little and whose brooding silence is interpreted by most Saulaeans as a sign of profound intelligence. He was to be our special sea investigator. I was glad of this because I am, to put it mildly, *afraid* of the sea.

Fiamuamua, our third investigator, had, as usual, manoeuvred his clever way on to our committee. He considers himself the most educated among us, having finished fifth form at Samoa College. However, we all know that his qualifications couldn't get him an office job in town and he had returned to Saula to pester us with his arrogant pretensions.

'What if the Bad Smell is being caused by *other* things?' Fiamuamua asked as soon as we were seated. He was already trying to take the leadership.

'What do you mean by *other*?' Tila asked.

'If it's *others*,' I interjected, 'we can deal with those too.' Fiamuamua tried to speak but I kept talking. 'But, firstly we will assume that the cause, or causes, of the Bad Smell are of this world.'

'As I see it,' Fiamuamua continued to attempt to usurp my leadership role, 'we should search the whole village first.' He stopped abruptly when he noted that the others weren't bothering to look at him, let alone listen to him.

'We will assemble all the taulele'a, divide them into

four groups, each to be led by one of us, divide the village into specific areas and assign each of them to the groups to search thoroughly,' I explained. Tila and Fa'afofoga nodded. Fiamuamua opened his mouth – and he had ugly teeth – to speak again. 'Do you agree?' I stopped his mouth.

I sent three of my sons to summon our men, and within thirty minutes they were in my large sitting room and I had divided them into four groups. (The group I assigned to Fiamuamua groaned audibly when I did so.)

I have a large blackboard which I use for teaching my children in the evenings. (I'm not a qualified teacher but my father and his father had been, so I am pursuing an aiga tradition.)

Quickly I drew a sketch map of our village on the blackboard. (Geography had been one of my strong subjects at high school.)

'That map isn't *quite* correct,' Fiamuamua said. No one paid him any attention.

On the map, I drew straight lines from the seashore through the village and into the plantations, dividing the village into four areas.

'We'll take one of the middle sections,' Fiamuamua offered – it was the least crowded area. No one looked at him. I chose his group to search the western area which is the rockiest and inhabited by rows of pig-sties and latrines. My group was allotted the middle area – after all, I *was* chairman.

'We'll all start in a line from the beach and work inland,' I instructed. Fiamuamua didn't nod, all the others did. 'As soon as you find a possible source, send someone to inform me.'

As we were leaving my house, we observed Fiamuamua folding a large red handkerchief and tying it around his nose and mouth – like a bandit in a cowboy film. 'To stop the Bad Smell,' he said through his mask. Some of us chuckled. 'It might be poisonous!' he argued.

Suddenly, we considered him wise for once, but, being the courageous men that we were, we refused to wear masks.

'If we get poisoned, we *get* poisoned!' Tila challenged the Bad Smell and Fiamuamua.

We searched every corner of our village for two futile, tiring hours. As was to be expected, Fiamuamua raised three false alarms that nearly choked us with heart-thundering hope as we all dashed to his sector to confront, firstly, a stand of dying banana trees, secondly an almost dry pile of turds (pardon the impoliteness), and lastly, with murder in our hearts, the almost fully decayed skeleton of a dog. The usually silent Fa'afofoga, his blazing eyes aimed like newly sharpened bush-knives at Fiamuamua, uttered his only comment for that afternoon: 'You do that again . . .' PAUSE . . . 'and . . .' PAUSE . . . 'and I will murder you!'

As we retreated tiredly to our respective homes, the Bad Smell smelled more infuriatingly nasty. We cursed It to ourselves, and like one of King Arthur's knights – I had read about them at high school – I swore a sacred vow that I would defeat the Bad Smell, even if it killed me.

After my aiga had gone to sleep, I circled, on my blackboard map, the area we had searched that after-noon. All around me the Bad Smell was a bristling thick sea of rottenness. The members of my aiga tossed and turned in their mosquito nets, and occasionally spat out their nausea. Most of them slept with their sleeping-sheets covering their faces.

The next morning, as arranged, our men gathered again at my house, after our morning meal. Many of them, like Fiamuamua, wore handkerchiefs as masks; most of them coughed constantly and spat out the phlegm; some looked sick. It was obvious that the Bad Smell was having detrimental effects on all of us.

Using my blackboard map, I divided the plantations into four equal areas, and assigned them to our groups.

My group got the flat fertile plain, which was green with large patches of taro and bananas.

'We will find its source today!' Fiamuamua vowed but no one else was *that* enthusiastically sure – we forgave him though: he had always been an optimist, though a tactlessly stupid one.

Reverend Lua, our revered pastor, was weeding in front of his house as my group and I went by.

'May God lead you to It today!' he called. We tried to smile hopefully and politely.

'Yes, I am sure God *will* lead us to It!' I replied.

We entered our assigned area, spread out in a straight line and started moving inland slowly, searching every tree, stone, stand of crops. Everything. Methodically.

'No one is to rest until I say so!' I ordered my men. 'No one!'

An hour or so later, our bodies sleek with sweat, our skins stinging from the heat, two of my men – elderly admittedly – sat down in the shade of a mango tree.

'We must not rest!' I called. 'Stand up!' Reluctantly, they followed me.

I noticed, slowly, that the Bad Smell was of an equal density everywhere, even when we penetrated deeper and deeper into the plantations. Within enclosed spaces, such as banana stands, the stinking thickness was the same. East, west, south, north – It was of equal nastiness, a thick transparent syrup.

Later, I experimented. I sent a youth up a tall palm tree. Every ten paces up the trunk, I asked him if the smell was the same. All the way to the top, he kept informing us that the Bad Smell was neither increasing nor decreasing in density. Even the soft breeze, which varied in strength and flow, was having no effect on that density.

Late that afternoon, too exhausted and hungry to be angry about the Bad Smell whose source we had once again failed to find, we reassembled in my house. No one, not even the usually loquacious Fiamuamua, said anything, as we ate the meal of stewed tinned herrings and umu-cooked taro and bananas that my aiga served us. No one was bothering with masks either. We didn't care if the offensive Smell was attacking us: only our empty bellies were important.

Afterwards, before my men could escape to their homes and inevitable sleep, I drew the inland boundary of that day's search on our blackboard map.

'Tomorrow we will search the bush immediately behind the plantations,' I instructed them. Silence. No one seemed to care.

'Sir, I can't come tomorrow, I have aiga problems to attend to,' said Tila, our most poetic group leader. Before I could push him back into line, three others were offering excuses.

'The council has entrusted us with a most important mission,' I threatened them. 'You, Tila, must *not* disappoint them. For the sake of our village, we *must* find the source of the Bad Smell!' Immediately, Tila reoffered his services; the others did too. I decided to be more vigilant (and ruthless) about any signs of indiscipline.

During our evening meal, I noted, with relief, that my children ate, laughed and argued as if the Bad Smell wasn't troubling them any more. I remembered my wise but strict father, telling me one day while we were out fishing for bonito, that we people got used, imperceptibly, to even the worst things given enough time and our need to survive. Were we getting accustomed to the Bad Smell?

We were about half a mile into the dense bush, the next morning, when my breath caught itself in my nostrils – the air was brilliantly fresh. I stepped two paces back, breathed in, the Bad Smell almost choked me. I stumbled two paces forward and was once again through the perimeter of the Bad Smell into the cool, laughing, invigorating freshness of the bush and hills.

We laughed and danced as we poked our heads in

and out of the Bad Smell, telling one another about the Edge, the dividing line between the Bad Smell and Freedom.

For about 500 yards we traced the Edge and decided that it ran in a line through the bush northwards and southwards.

I have always been blessed with a very astute, sometimes profound intuitive sight, which in unexpected moments brought me lucid glimpses into the so-called mysteries of ordinary life. Such a glimpse opened my mind as we were hurrying back to our village to tell everyone about the Bad Smell's inland Edge. The Bad Smell has a corresponding sea perimeter, the message registered in my head. That being so, It must therefore have northern and southern boundaries.

I didn't tell anyone though.

That night, I drew the bush perimeter on our blackboard map.

'What does it mean?' my mother asked me after I had explained the Edge.

'Yes, what?' my wife asked, equally afraid.

'Must be like the film I saw last year at the Tivoli in Apia.' Siaki stirred their fear. 'The Blob, it was called. About this huge horrible blob that settled over a whole village in Japan and sucked up all the electricity, houses, people. Everything into Its evil body!'

'What happened to It?' our mother asked him, giving me the opportunity to cure their fear.

'It died!' I laughed and our children laughed too.

Using a fleet of alia with outboard motors we searched the sea within the reef the next morning, and, as I had expected, we found that the Bad Smell had a sea perimeter. Beyond it, the air smelled of tingling salt and brisk sun and wind. 'Like a willing, fertile woman!' Fa'afofoga described it.

We sucked it in as we lay in our canoes, our hands trailing in the diamond-blue water, chuckling, sighing, gazing up into heavens as huge as a child's imagination.

Strangely, we didn't mind returning into the Bad Smell and our village, knowing that there were limits to our prison out of which we could escape any moment we chose to.

During lotu that night, my mother thanked the Almighty for having revealed to us, His helpless children, the dividing line between Evil (the Bad Smell) and the saving air of Goodness. I hadn't thought of it that way but I had to agree with her. Confronted with our common problem and adversary, my mother was acquiring *some* wisdom.

I waited until my aiga were asleep then I drew in the sea perimeter, and sat down in front of our blackboard and contemplated my map. Mentally, I filled in the northern and southern perimeters. The insight blinked like the opening of a bright eye, and I saw it: the whole area *occupied* (that was the appropriate description) by the Bad Smell was oval-shaped and our church building was its centre.

Silently I made my way through the still darkness and our sleeping village, that came alive periodically with the familiar sucking sound of the cicadas, to our church, expecting the up-thrusting currents of the Bad Smell to be streaming up from its foundations and the very earth on which it stood, knowing from what my grandfather had told me as a boy that the missionaries had deliberately sited the church on the centre of our malae where, during pagan times, prisoners of war had been killed and sometimes cooked and eaten.

I found no up-surging fountain of foulness. Just the massive sinews of concrete and stone and corrugated iron caught in the ocean that was the Bad Smell.

In the next two days, we located, and drew on our map, the northern and southern boundaries.

'An oval!' exclaimed Fiamuamua before I could tell everyone that I knew *that* already.

'Like a gigantic egg!' Tila said, poetically. 'Like the egg of the Roc, which Sinbad the Sailor discovered.'

And, before I could distract him, he was telling that tale to an attentive audience, who had demanded that he tell it.

I tried to be patient: leaders *have* to be patient with the weaknesses of their followers. There was no way, short of an angry demand from me, to break Tila's spell. We were all suckers, so a papalagi would say, for fantastic stories, fairy tales; and Sinbad's adventures were a rich strand of our village's mythology.

While Tila wove his magic, I realized that we didn't really care any more about the Bad Smell's source: we had been pre-occupied almost totally with mapping It. Perhaps there was no source? But It must have come from somewhere? Another lucid insight opened in the centre of my head: perhaps It has always been here in our village in another dimension, and some slight alteration in our existence had sucked that dimension into our daily lives? My imagination was running away with me; I stopped my thoughts. You may as well believe in Siaki's incredible story of the Red Blob!

'How high is the Bad Smell's outer perimeter?' The usually silent Fa'afofoga fished me out of my head.

'If we had a plane, we could find out!' said Fiamuamua.

'A helicopter!' added someone else.

'What's that?' someone asked.

Before the fickle imaginations of my men could be distracted again, I said, firmly, 'Here is what we have discovered so far about our friend the Bad Smell!' I now had their attention. 'Firstly, we still don't know Its source.' Pause. Pointed at the map. 'Secondly, we don't know, because we don't have a helicopter, how high It rises.' Pause. 'Thirdly, we don't know if It penetrates into the ground and, if It does, how far down it goes.' I was surprised by that sudden insight. 'Yes,' I re-emphasized, 'It *must* have a downward perimeter!' Even Fiamuamua nodded. 'So if we are all agreed on the boundaries of the Bad Smell, this is how It might look.'

I went up to the blackboard and, with bold yellow chalk, drew these diagrams:

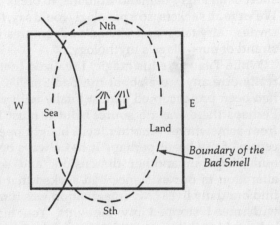

*Looking down at the Bad Smell*

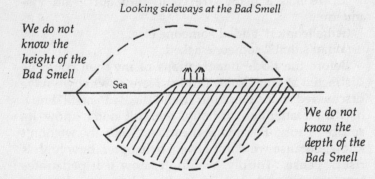

*Looking sideways at the Bad Smell*

The geography and maths I had studied at high school had come in useful, I concluded, admiring my diagrams.

'Perhaps It extends right up to Heaven where our God dwells.' The profound Faafofoga eased his wise presence into our contemplation.

'Perhaps It also extends down to hell where Satan dwells,' Fiamuamua speculated pessimistically, and frightened us.

'Our village is the yellow of the Roc's Egg that is the shape and form of the Bad Smell,' Tila described slowly. Looking again at my diagrams we had to agree with Tila – and I resented him somewhat for having seen that symbolic truth before I had.

In every community there is always that hard-hearted realist who, whenever our imaginations lift us up into dizzy poetic speculations, drags us back down to our body odour and juices and pain.

'That is all very well,' my wife's intimidating voice started clipping off our dazzling, speculative wings, 'but do you yet know what the Bad Smell is, why It is here, and how you are going to get rid of It?' Before I could stop her interference, she added, 'In short, how are we, the bright yellow of the Roc's Egg, going to hatch ourselves out of that Egg and breathe fresh air again?'

All my men looked at me to save them from my wife's large, unwelcomed truth. Blank spaces punched at my frantic search for an answer.

'It's time we fed these hungry men!' I ordered her. As she whirled to go and bring our meal, I caught an infuriating glint of triumph in her eyes. My men tried not to look at me; they didn't envy me my brilliantly perceptive spouse and the defeat she had just inflicted on me without justification. Right then, I envied them their extremely obedient wives who never revealed – at least in public – how dumb (or otherwise) their husbands were. Not the time for senseless domestic quarrels, we had a formidable enemy to defeat, I soothed my pride.

Sunday. Reverend Lua's particularly forceful sermon in the morning service can be summed up thus:

*Text*: 'The Bad Smell is punishment from our wrathful, just God because we have sinned!'

*Body*: 'For almost one arduous, trying year, he, Lua, had tried his humble, utmost best to warn us of our wicked, sinful ways. For instance, on New Year's Day, ten disobedient, hypocritical matai and fifteen wicked, greedy taulele'a had spent the day carousing at one of Apia's sinful, expensive beer clubs; eleven of them had been jailed after the huge, violent brawl which had wrecked that heathen, unchristian club; and he, God's humble, worthless servant had been forced to plead with the police to release the worthless, licentious brawlers.' (Licentious because unmentionable, wanton sisters of Salome had featured prominently in the brawl.) (*Aside:* I note here, as I report this, that the learned Reverend Lua uses double adjectives to describe almost every noun he uses; I must learn that.)

'A slow restful month later, a shameless, aigaless matai, who was to remain anonymous, brought irreparable, painful shame to our peaceful, honest village by going to jail for stealing food from an important, innocent papalagi's house in Apia. Lo and behold, just as we were recovering from that unpardonable, disgraceful disgrace, three of our youths were gaoled for killing and eating someone else's well-looked-after, well-fed pig.'

Reverend Lua, a small man whose crisp speech and jerky tense movements remind me of a fit rooster with gas in its belly, then proceeded to enumerate and condemn another gallery of rogues, criminals and sinners. The most colourful cases concerned: a hinted-at adultery between an unnamed but satanic matai and an unnamed but promiscuous girl who was now living in another unnamed village; a stone-hearted, pagan aiga (which had since converted to that unholy, unmention-able sect called Mormonism – a sin in itself!), who had in a satan-inspired, blind anger almost castrated ('oper-ated on' was Lua's polite term) a youth who had, secretly, but knowingly, impregnated one of their innocent, godly daughters; and most revolting of all was the beastly act between an obviously insane, two-legged beast and an innocent, unaware four-legged one.

Though the rogues were not named by the honest, forthright Reverend Lua, he knew that we all knew who they were.

*Conclusion of Rev. Lua's Sermon:* 'So because of all our unpardonable, vicious sins, God, who is a just and loving Father, has now shrouded us in an invisible, strangling shroud of Rottenness and Decay. To be free from It we must repent, ask Him for His boundless, all-embracing forgiveness . . .'

He finished by encouraging us to pray fervently to God for His forgiveness, that night, which all our aiga did, then we slept soundly, expecting God's forgiveness to descend on Monday morning.

At dawn I woke; we were still in the embrace of the Bad Smell, and I cursed myself and our people for not having repented genuinely enough. The Almighty, I am sure, would have forgiven us otherwise.

On Wednesday, I spent a long time mentally compos-ing the verbal report I was expected to give to the matai council the next day. I would also show them my neat blackboard map and diagrams.

For half an hour or so I mesmerized the council like the cobras I had seen in an Indian film. 'We are liv-ing in the Roc's Egg,' I concluded my speech, using Tila's imagery. 'Soon we will, with God's help, hatch from It!'

Obviously impressed, Pesemalie, our tu'ua, thanked me and my men, profusely, then in his practical wisdom, he said, 'You have mapped out the Enemy, now tell us Its source and how we are going to rid ourselves of It.'

'We do not, as yet, know the source,' I apologized, 'and, because of that, we cannot recommend ways of destroying it.'

Fiamuamua recommended a further fervent appeal to God for his divine intervention.

'And if prayers don't work again?' Pesemalie asked. For once, the loquacious Fiamuamua was without words. 'Let us all sit here quietly and think of a cure,' Pesemalie suggested. 'God, I am sure, will whisper the answer to us!'

We sat and we thought. We sat and we thought. Desperately, I wanted my usually faithful intuition to flash me the answer. Alas, no answer came.

'. . . There is a man, a man who *has* cures.' Fa'afofoga our expert fisherman hooked us out of our drowning. We waited for it, impatiently. 'Cures for Samoan diseases, aitu diseases,' he added. Long pause as he pondered the fale's ceiling. 'I once witnessed his powers – he cured a cripple who had been crippled all his sad life.' Another lengthy pause.

'Get on with it!' Pesemalie voiced our impatience.

'. . . And once a leper and a madman . . .'

'Yes, but what about bad smells, and bad smells of our size?' Pesemalie hurried him.

'Not bad smells,' Fa'afofoga admitted quietly.

'You and your leader [meaning me] will go and consult him anyway,' ordered Pesemalie. 'Tell him our problem and see if he can do something about it.'

'Perhaps we should consult a papalagi scientist in Apia at the Agriculture Department?' Fiamuamua suggested.

'Afterwards!' Pesemalie dismissed him.

I consider myself a modern and educated man. I therefore have little faith in traditional medicines and healers, especially healers who claim they can cure maladies caused by aitu, but I wasn't going to disobey Pesemalie.

To my surprise, Fa'afofoga's miracle healer, or taulasea, did not live in a traditional village but in the middle of Apia, in a shabby, ramshackled neighbourhood called the Vaipe, Dead-Water, an appropriate name. Ironical for that most urbanized neighbourhood to produce what Fa'afofoga, on our bumpy way to Apia on the bus, had described reverently as 'a very wise and saintly taulasea who knows all the aitu and the illnesses they can cause'.

Vavega, the taulasea, is a decrepit wisp of an old man (more sagging skin and bone than flesh) who is almost totally blind and needs to be led everywhere by his daughter. He welcomed us, and his aiga served us a breakfast of hot tea and buttered bread.

While we ate, Fa'afofoga told him why we had come.

'This Bad Smell, how extensive is It?' he asked.

Methodically, I explained everything I knew about It. Vavega nodded periodically, the wisp of white hair on the top of his almost bald head reminded me of cigarette smoke.

'No source, no reason for Its visitation – very puzzling!' he exclaimed. Though his physical presence was like a whisper, his spiritual essence, or mana, was thickening, as it were, for me. My admiration and respect deepened. 'Its density is the same everywhere?'

'Yes,' I replied eagerly. (How did he know?)

'Very mysterious!' he muttered. 'I will come and try and defeat It!' We thanked him. 'We will come tomorrow morning – my daughter and I.'

As we stepped out of his shack, his daughter, a massive matron with small delicate hands and generous eyes, stopped us. 'My father is very frail now, we *have* to travel by taxi.'

I gave her $10 which she accepted politely. 'Our village is ready to pay all your expenses,' I said.

'All we want is for your kind father to drive the Bad Smell from our humble village!' Fa'afofoga said.

'We will arrive at mid-morning,' she said. 'You will provide us with a house. No one else must live there while we are there. My father must have total privacy in order to work properly. Your village must also *act* as if we aren't there. There will be no welcome ceremonies and so on.' She paused and looked at us in turn. 'If he defeats the Bad Smell you will deposit in his bank account, $200. If he fails, no payment will be made. You must never mention money or expenses to him. He is too spiritual for that. He is an old man, and I must protect *his* interests. He does not believe in selling his gift, but we are a poor aiga.'

'We understand,' I replied, impressed. 'We will obey your every wish.'

That night the matai council accepted my generous offer for Vavega and his daughter to use my papalagi house which was, according to Pesemalie, the most luxurious house in our district, and therefore most appropriate accommodation for our important guests. (My two sons and one daughter in New Zealand had sent money for the house.) While Vavega and his daughter were in our house, my aiga and I would live in our two fale.

As is the custom, each aiga was to feed our guests for a day; only the best food was to be served.

It is difficult, anywhere, for people who are bursting with curiosity to pretend that a well-known healer of supernatural diseases is *not* in their midst investigating such a freak phenomenon as the Bad Smell. But we tried, meticulously.

For instance, no one else came out to greet them when they arrived by taxi at our house on Wednesday; I took them in, showed them where everything was and then left them alone. None of the matai came; everyone kept away from the house, and all who went past behaved as if the house wasn't there. Their lunch was brought by two people of the appointed aiga and left in the sitting room for Vavega's daughter to serve.

All day I remained in our fale, writing long letters to my children in New Zealand, describing the Bad Smell but not mentioning Vavega. Occasionally I glimpsed Vavega shuffling round the sitting room where I had deliberately left my blackboard with its maps and diagrams of the Bad Smell. Once, he stopped and peered at the blackboard, nodding his bird-like head as though saying, yes, yes, yes.

No one said much during our evening meal, no one dared look at our house, but as soon as the children were ready for bed, some of them sneaked out and, creeping up to the house, sat at the edge of the light being cast from the sitting room and watched Vavega who was slumped in a chair, pondering my diagrams, trying desperately to untangle the riddle of the Bad Smell so we could be hatched. From the secure darkness of our fale, I observed him, my sleeping-sheet wrapped like a second skin around me. The whole neighbourhood, I sensed, were doing the same thing. Vavega was the fire, we were those seeking its warmth, its healing.

He sat and pondered, sat and pondered, for a long, long time. The village lights went out one by one, and left me alone with Vavega. He started nodding with sleep. Vavega's daughter appeared from the kitchen and helped him off to bed. A few minutes later, the house was in darkness.

Once again, the Bad Smell invaded my consciousness. We were trapped in a dead egg.

For four days, Vavega and his daughter, with our consent, moved with a quiet, undisturbed invisibility through our village and its immediate environs. I observed, surreptitiously, their every move, gathering detailed information from other people, including our children, and each night recording it in my thick, black notebook.

I have already described their first day (Wednesday); here are my notebook entries for their next three days. (By the way, V in my notes is Vavega, and D is his daughter.)

*Thursday*
V.D. are up early. V is on the back veranda gargling loudly and spitting the water on to the grass. V, who is dressed in an old lavalava and ragged singlet, then parts his lavalava and makes water on to the grass. D is in the kitchen cooking. V shuffles back into the house.

For thirty minutes I watch but nothing happens. Then V.D. leave the house through the front door, he is leaning his left hand on her strong shoulder, his right hand is with a steel walking-stick that he stabs into the ground, as they walk slowly towards the centre of our village.

I wait but they don't return until midday. She is holding him up, with her arm around his waist. (I stop myself from rushing out and helping them.) His eyes are closed, he is breathing heavily, she takes him and puts him to bed. They don't leave the house the whole of this afternoon. According to ten reliable eyewitnesses I questioned this afternoon, V.D. went into our church first and D sat in a back pew, praying, while V went around checking every nook and cranny of the building, using his shiny steel walking-stick to tap at everything. One witness said, 'It appeared to my humble self that Mr V was *listening* to the sounds that his stick was making.'

After a thorough inspection of the innards of the church, V.D. then inspected the outside, especially the ground at the foot of the massive walls, this time, D stabbed the steel walking-stick into the ground – at least a foot down each time – whenever V told her to, and V, after D pulled it out, examined the dirt that was on the stick. According to one witness: 'Mr V, with his fingers, would scrape some of the dirt off the stick, rub it

116

between his fingers and then sniff at it.' One child reported that he even saw V taste some of the dirt with the tip of his tongue.

## Night

After their evening meal, V.D. leave the house and disappear into the village. I time their absence on the gold wrist-watch my eldest son sent me as an Xmas gift last year. V.D. are away until 11.55 p.m., when everyone else is asleep. Once again, I note with concern, but I can't help him, V's state of exhaustion as D half-carries him into the house and bed.

## Friday

I wake at dawn. No sign of anyone in the house so I creep up and look in. No one.

They return, and D is looking strong and cheerful, as we are having our morning meal. Before they go into the house, he waves his walking-stick to us. Automatically just about my whole aiga, including your humble servant, wave back and then feel stupid suddenly because we are not supposed to be watching V.D.

As I watch the house this morning I no longer doubt V's powers, though my education keeps telling me that I shouldn't have faith in taulasea.

V.D. leave at mid-morning and go to the beach, with D holding a black umbrella over V. They do not return until 1 p.m., with D once again half-carrying him.

They sleep the whole afternoon. It is raining strongly this evening and I can only reach five eyewitnesses to V.D.'s movements that morning.

V.D. had spent that time exploring the whole length of beach, with D once again using V's walking-stick to stab into the sand and under the rocks and driftwood, and provide samples of dirt for V to feel, smell and taste.

One witness said, 'On their way back, Mr V found a smooth patch of wet sand and, using a short piece of wood, drew your (meaning your humble servant) egg diagram of the Bad Smell in the sand.'

'What else happened?' I asked.

'Nothing, he just erased it with his foot, a few minutes later.'

'How did he look?'

'Very upset, almost in tears!'

As I gaze into the rain that is washing the night but is unable to clean it of the Bad Smell, I think sadly of V.

*Saturday*

As usual I wake at dawn. There is no movement in the house but I don't feel the urgent need to discover what is happening there. When my wife wakes a short while later I describe to her the strange dream I had experienced that night. Here are my words:

'I am afloat in a sea as green as young grass, looking up into an egg-yellow sky. The water feels like feathers. Suddenly above me the yellow cracks open noiselessly as if something or someone is pulling it apart, and I feel myself being sucked up into the black opening by a wind which I can't feel but which I can hear whistling and swishing and sighing. Before I reach the jagged edge of the opening, I find Vavega's steel walking-stick in my hands, it is glowing like a light bulb and feels hot but not hot enough to burn my hands. I think of Cinderella's fairy godmother and her magic wand that changed a pumpkin into a golden coach and mice into white stallions and Cinderella into a beautiful princess with glass slippers. And I point Vavega's wand at my heart and, without an ounce of pain, stab it in, down until all of me is glowing like a phosphorescent light bulb. I am outside myself looking at the dazzling figure that I am. There is a sudden hush, an abyss of endless silence that, within frightening seconds, is contracting around my skin like a steel shell. I am choking. 'You will be our saviour!' Vavega's voice whispers in my ear.

(I can't remember which ear.) And I burst out of my smothering steel shell. I wake up watching a smiling Vavega in red robes and turban (like a prophet in the Bible), shrinking steadily until he is nothing.'

'I will be our saviour!' I repeat to my wife. 'Vavega believes in my mission.'

'What mission?' she asks incredulously.

'Nothing.' She won't understand.

'He is going to fail, isn't he?' she asks.

'Vavega?'

'Yes.'

Right then the meaning of my precious dream revealed itself to me: Vavega wasn't going to defeat the Bad Smell but, in my sleep, using his mysterious powers (mental telepathy, the papalagi call it), he had made me his heir, his knight who was to continue the war against the evil smell and conquer It. 'He may still succeed,' I lie to my wife.

I go to the house a short while later. I enter it without knocking. I search it. There is no evidence that V.D. were ever there. Invisible they had come and invisible they had left.

On the blackboard printed in frail yellow letters under my egg diagram is this message from V:

YOUR MAPS AND DIAGRAMS OF YOUR BAD SMELL ARE VERY ACCURATE. YOUR BAD SMELL IS AN EGG. CONGRATULATIONS ON YOUR DISCOVERY. BUT IT IS ONE THING TO ACCURATELY MAP OUT THE SHAPE AND SIZE OF EVIL AND IT IS ANOTHER TO DESTROY IT.

I HAVE FAILED.

As I hurried to Pesemalie's fale to inform him of Vavega's failure, my whole being was swimming with joy at Vavega entrusting me with the divine mission. If he had succeeded, the purpose of my existence would have been lost.

Pesemalie summoned a council meeting immediately and told them: 'The taulasea has left admitting he can't defeat the Bad Smell. He tried his best but he is very old, no longer with the necessary mana. What shall we do now?'

'Sir, perhaps, with your kind permission, we should seek the help of a scientist?' Fiamuamua offered.

When the council agreed to that, I experienced a sharp hatred for Fiamuamua, believing that he was trying to deny me the right to save our village, but I hid my feelings well – I even offered my house for the scientist.

Fiamuamua went to Apia and, a day later, rode like a conqueror into our village in a blue Land-Rover, with a Mr Trevor Mellows from the Agriculture Department.

The council gathered in Pesemalie's fale to give the papalagi a ceremonial welcome, as is the custom, but the papalagi, who is a spindly man with fire-orange hair and freckles and thin hairy legs, refused to waste time with ceremony. Cleverly, Fiamuamua interpreted politely, to the council, the papalagi's rude refusal.

The papalagi and his three aides, long-haired youths in jeans, spread out large copies of my maps and diagrams, which Fiamuamua had provided them without my permission, on the hood of their Land-Rover, and, with Fiamuamua's boastful help, identified all the landmarks and areas, then the papalagi issued orders to his aides and they all dispersed in various directions, with Fiamuamua following the papalagi like a hungry puppy.

I wanted nothing to do with their attempt; they were going to fail and I didn't want to be tainted by that aroma. Let the deserving Fiamuamua take all of it!

I spent the day repairing our kitchen fale. After the papalagi and his crew had departed for Apia at 4.30 p.m. precisely, I went round gathering information about what nearly everyone was now referring to seriously as 'Fiamuamua's papalagi and his scientific research'.

Here is a brief summary of that information which I later recorded in my notebook:

'The papalagi and his men filled small jars with soil samples dug up from various locations within the area covered by the Bad Smell and just outside Its perimeter. They also took samples of water found within the Bad Smell. The papalagi questioned a cross-section of our people, with the upstart Fiamuamua acting as his interpreter, about animals, crops, diseases and so on. Everyone reported that the papalagi refused to eat our food or drink our water.'

When the papalagi and his crew did not return the next day, Fiamuamua boasted to us, 'He will bring his answers tomorrow, wait and see!'

They did return on Saturday, but not with any answers, but to take samples of the air, the sea-water, our crops and other plants.

Reverend Lua's lucid Sunday-morning sermon emphasized the astounding power of modern science, describing in fervent, vivid detail such scientific miracles as heart transplants, nuclear bombs, Disneyland, space flight, and the thirty-five different flavours of ice cream which he had tasted in Los Angeles, when he had visited his children the previous year. We envied him his knowledge of such wonders, and especially his visit to Disneyland. Nevertheless he concluded by saying, 'However, science, without belief in God, is unholy. Science can explain much, but only our all-seeing God can explain everything!'

Fiamuamua's over-confidence deflated visibly when Monday came and passed without any sign of his papalagi and his papalagi's answers. When the same thing happened on Tuesday Fiamuamua hid in his house, and early on Wednesday morning he sneaked into a bus and disappeared into Apia obviously to look for his papalagi, his passport back into our favour.

All day Wednesday we waited. That night I told the other matai that papalagi science was failing us, which led Pesemalie to remark: 'What do you expect from atheists [meaning the papalagi]?' 'What do you expect from half-educated boys [meaning Fiamuamua]?'

As I gazed that night at my maps and diagrams, a bubbling stream of joy washed through me. The Roc's Egg had defeated traditional healing and now modern science; it was once again up to me.

While all these events, which I have described so far, were occurring, the notoriety (fame) of the Bad Smell and our humble village spread, like a flood, throughout our humble country. Those of our people who were branded by Pesemalie as 'weak noses and soft stomachs' fled out of the egg, taking their exaggerated prejudices against our Bad Smell (and our village) to taint other people. 'It is good they have gone,' said Pesemalie, 'my ears were tired of their complaints and fears!'

The national response to our Odour was various. Religious fundamentalists labelled our innocent village a den of sin, a Gomorrah; the Bad Smell was our punishment. The educated were, like Fiamuamua's papalagi, interested in the natural, scientific causes of our Odour; some even visited, took samples, and went home and tried to find solutions. The merely curious – and they were the most numerous and included foreign tourists – drove slowly through our village, some holding perfumed handkerchiefs to their noses as they examined us, as though we were helpless specimens trapped in our most peculiar environment. One national leader, originally a doctor, sent a Health Department team to see if we needed some form of inoculation. The superstitious and ignorant talked of aitu, sauali'i, demons and the Dead rising up to take their revenge.

Our responses to the varied national response were equally various. Reverend Lua and many of us were highly elated at the attention we were attracting – the national radio station even broadcast a series of news items about our Odour. The realists, like my wife, refused to be euphoric, and got fed up with the strangers who were visiting us. As my wife put it: 'Why can't they leave us and our Smell alone?' Our fundamentalists, led by Reverend Lua, worshipped together in our church with a group of foreign fundamentalists they had invited and then they lunched together at our expense (we are well-known for our generous hospitality), in Reverend Lua's large house. Our scientifically minded, such as Fia-muamua, after the papalagi scientist's failure, refused to be hospitable to their foreign counterparts who came to experiment with us. (Fiamuamua, fearful of our wrath, absented himself from our council meetings.) Our super-stitious ones welcomed their foreign counterparts and they spent long hours echoing one another's superstitious interpretations of our Smell.

Only I stood above these biases, prejudices, false posturings, etc. I was the true guardian of our village and our Smell; only I in my objectivity could save us.

Soon after Fiamuamua's failure – and I relished his loss of standing in our community – Pesemalie, at our next council meeting, argued, quite persuasively and correctly, that as long as we couldn't get rid of our Bad Smell we had to persuade our nation that we hadn't caused It, or even more wisely, that it was a harmless, non-infectious and healthy odour, a mark of distinction and uniqueness. 'I mean, what other village in this arrogant country in this vast ocean on our sinful planet possesses such a unique smell?' he argued convincingly.

We all agreed to this truth and went home and instructed our aiga to spread it far and wide. For this campaign, I coined a very original slogan: OUR SMELL IS THE PERFUME OF THE PACIFIC; IT IS THE SCENT OF BIRTH. Our leading song-maker used it in a song which became a national hit after our village choir, the Ai-Ulu-Moto (Eaters of Immature Breadfruit), sang it at last year's national Independence Celebrations at Mulinu'u.

It is over a year now since our Bad Smell (or, more properly, our Odour) first visited us (or, should I say, *revealed* itself to us?). Apart from me, no one is bothering to discuss It, or find cures for It, any more. Most of us lack the stamina, the dedication, the commitment, the passion for the fight. We don't even bother with the curious visitors who come to experience It now. Occasionally we are roused to a vengeful, fierce anger if someone insults us by flaunting in our faces our now nationally known nickname, 'Saula and the Stench'. Wouldn't you get angry?

But apart from these moments of fire, we acknowledge our Odour as an essential part of our lives as if It has always been here since our village was founded hundreds of years ago. 'It is the air we breathe!' Pesemalie has described It, profoundly.

The other night I asked my aiga, 'Can you still smell It?' They looked blankly at me.

I refuse to give up. Secretly I have tried to devise ways to hatch ourselves out of the Egg. My satchel is full of my diagrams of these stillborn solutions. Most representative of them are these ones:

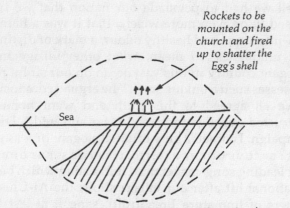

Rockets to be mounted on the church and fired up to shatter the Egg's shell

Sea

*(Alas, I have not been able to procure the rockets)*

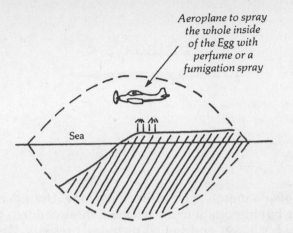

*Aeroplane to spray the whole inside of the Egg with perfume or a fumigation spray*

Sea

*(Alas, I don't have the money to hire a plane and buy the eighteen tons of perfume needed.)*

In between my scientific experimentation, I have spent my time writing, in accurate detail, all that has happened since we first became conscious of our Odour. If something happens to me before we are hatched, my written records will provide whoever is brave and committed enough to continue the valiant struggle with solid, scientific data on which to base his strategies. Not that my life is to end shortly. The Almighty in my sleep last night whispered to me that He is granting me a long life.

You may well ask: But if all your people are now living quite happily with your Odour and don't see the need to be saved from It why are you, a weak mortal, still trying to save them from It?

My reply to that is: Sinbad the Sailor's adventures and quests were the justification for his existence. Similarly, my struggle, my mission, is the meaning of my life. I was born for it.

I will be our saviour. God has willed it so.

# Birthdays

Just over a month ago I turned forty-one. Unimportant to me but important to my wife and three children who enjoy birthdays and giving birthday presents. Unlike them, I never had a birthday party until I had reached the age of twenty-one. (My parents, when I was a boy, were 'poor', and it isn't fa'a-Samoa to celebrate birthdays every year.)

For my twenty-first party, a friend and I went into a bottle store in Wellington to buy the liquor. It was to be the first time I would be in a pub *legally*, so we breezed in, exuding over-confidence. (My friend wasn't yet twenty-one.)

The barman scrutinized me and asked what I wanted. I started reeling off the list.

'Sorry, mate!' he stopped me. 'But you can't buy anything here.'

'Why?' I replied, angry and convinced I was confronting another racist.

'Are you twenty-one?'

'I turned twenty-one two days ago!' I insisted.

'Sorry, mate. Unless you have proof that you're twenty-one, I can't serve you.' There was an infuriating smile on his face. 'I can serve your mate though,' he said. '*He* looks twenty-one!'

I wasn't going to argue. So my mate, who was not yet a manly twenty-one, ordered and paid for our liquor with the money I, the under twenty-one-looking twenty-one, gave him under the nose of our alert and perceptive barman.

As we staggered out of the bottle store with our burden of liquor, my friend laughed uproariously while I fumed, insulted that I didn't yet look a man. However, as we drove in a cab to our flat, I thought about it, and my vanity won out – I would always look younger than my years. (Even today, I believe I look ten years younger than I am. Vanity, all is vanity!)

My birthday party was a rip-roaring affair at my cousin's home at Wainuiomata. Uncle Tunupopo, my mother's brother, came from Samoa for it, bringing my father's present – a portable typewriter and the first and only visible proof that he didn't mind me trying to be a writer. (He had wanted me – and was still hoping for me – to be a lawyer, a creature considered by most of our people as occupying a rank next to God! Not knowing what I wanted to be I had drifted into Teachers' Training College, then to university, spending much of my time trying to write poems and stories.)

Uncle Tunupopo, who was named after my great-grandfather Asi Tunupopo, a notorious warrior and womanizer, spoke at my birthday, and the chilling blessing he conferred publicly on me was the Samoan proverb: 'May your path be paved with blood!' This was the traditional blessing given to young warriors before they went into battle. (I've used more ink than blood since then, and prefer that!)

For my one and only birthday party I got a load of high-class ashtrays, cigarette lighters and books. At that time, I was a chain-smoker and aspiring (visibly and over-self-consciously) to being a writer after the unholy image of Dylan Thomas and Jim Baxter, the former a poet dying from being a public alcoholic, the latter a cured alcoholic and a convert to Roman Catholicism. Both were torrents of volcanically furious and magical words and imagery.

Since that portable typewriter, my father, though I give him the first copies of all my books, has never said to me what he thinks of my writing. From what people report to me, though, my father is proud of 'my son, the writer'. He should be because, in this status-hungry nation, his son's (the writer's) fame and notoriety are of higher status than any lawyer he had wanted his son to be.

Often when I'm with him (he's a very youthful-looking seventy-four now), I sense, as he examines me from his solid silence, that he still wishes I *had* become a respectable lawyer and church deacon. I stopped going to church many years ago, and my father has been hurt about it ever since, though I'm sure he believes that I will one day return from the cold. After all, I can't be all that pagan: I allow my children, his grandchildren, to go to Sunday School and church every Sunday. My father nearly wept with joy the Sunday Sina, my elder daughter, was confirmed in church. (Sina had chosen confirmation; we had left it to her.)

Very few fathers ever come to the disquieting realization that their sons *do* age into men who are older than twelve years old. My aristocratic father is not one of them. And, accepting this, I've learned to appreciate his complex depths and shallows, his extremely pragmatic world that is based on not taking risks or allowing yourself to dream visions that pull you beyond earth's gravity, a lifestyle that is governed by a belief in thrift, cleanliness, Godliness, hard work, and unquestioning loyalty to aiga and blood and your matai – I've never known my father to be anything else but supreme head of our aiga!

I love him, knowing that there are now more things left unsaid between us than the things we talk about: the silences that are better left unvoiced. I used to find these silences unrelentingly painful, and I'm sure he did too. Now they have become part of our relationship, as natural as saying hello to each other.

My father is a self-made man who does not believe in owing anyone anything, least of all money. I've always felt unable to live up to his solidity, his integrity, his faith in God and himself.

But once upon a time he was not of this planet, so to speak. Before I was born, he had become a well-known church organist and composer of church music; he trained many village church choirs, teaching them the hymns he composed. While he was choirmaster at the village of Vaiala, he met my mother and married her.

When I came into his world, he wasn't an active choirmaster any more; he composed hymns, and the youths who came to stay with us to learn how to play the organ taught the hymns to their village choirs. One of his nephews he trained to be a very proficient musician, and that nephew took over his role as composer and choirmaster, finally. This shedding of his gift occurred as he devoted more and more time to his plumbing business. That was about thirty years ago. Today he can't play the organ or piano. However, there is a piano in his sitting room; and, whenever I observe him listening to music on his enormous radio, I sense he can't separate his youth from his gift for music – the pain of knowing that he had once possessed that gift must be like an incorrigible guilt.

Because he gave up his talent, I sometimes think that that is part of the reason for my unquenchable desire to write, at any cost. All his children have done well educationally, and are as affluent as he is. The successes we have become are what he worked for. But at times I believe that he is proud that I've persisted in my refusal to relinquish my talent for rebellion and subversion. In his self-made honour, he lives with the pain of the musician he was and could have been. I blame myself and my brothers and sisters and our aiga for that price: he lived for us, to feed us well and get us the education he hadn't had: 'You can't feed anyone on music!' he would say in moments of exasperation. His was a sacrificial mutilation.

Today, every year on his birthday, he receives presents from his children and grandchildren and the relatives he helped to educate, feed and send abroad. He stores most of these gifts in his wardrobe and the fat metal chest, which he has carried from his childhood with him, content, at least for another year, that the heirs he sold his talent for still remember and value him and his sacrifice.

Some Sunday mornings I switch on the radio and hear hymns he has composed. As I listen, pride surges up in me, like the whole eternal song that is my childhood, to fill the limits of my breath, and I tell my wife and children to listen to the hymns of my father's youth. Sometimes I sing along with the choir, and am surprised that I still remember many of the verses. My children can't quite reconcile their stern grandfather with his generously beautiful songs. I hope one day they will realize the enormous sacrifice their grandfather made for his children and aiga.

And love him even more.

Last Saturday night, Mele, my second daughter, celebrated her thirteenth birthday with a noisy, food-and-music-rich party, and fifteen friends. I wrote her a birthday letter. Here it is:

### A Birthday Letter to Mele

In between a bossy sister (your description) and a demanding brother (my description), you've always felt squeezed out of your parents' affection. And when Sina and Michael torment you with the obvious fact I've not written a poem for you or about you, your blazing eyes accuse me of not loving you. What you don't realize is that poems are hard to come by; they don't grow in my hair or inside my rib-cage; they have to be fished out of the void like rare tunes or almost indecipherable messages from outer space.

But it's your thirteenth birthday and you're hungry for a poem, token of my love for you. I'll try not to flatter you.

Everyone and everything else does that, even the sunlight that makes your golden hair and skin glow like a sunset; and the waters of the still lagoon that echo the diamond blue-green of your eyes; and the eternal memory of a noble great-grandmother whose sacred name you bear; and the secret diary you keep as a record of your hurts and the torment you believe we are inflicting on you.

Despite your constant protests, things have always come easy to you, and you'll continue to charm your way through life, with pleasant ease. That's to be your weakness because you'll probably never have to realize the depths and power you're capable of. Who knows, though, I may be under-estimating the range of your vision, your sensitivity to your own profound depths and your strength to undergo suffering. Some jealous people will describe you as being 'just a pretty face'. Every time you gaze into a mirror or into other people's eyes, your own physical beauty gazes back at you. You *are* a beautiful face, and one day – and I hope it's soon – you'll have to search behind that for who you really are. I know you'll find some of your great-grandmother's indestructible bones there, some of your father's sick jokes, your mother's enduring love, and the rich skeleton that is your Samoan/Pakeha ancestry. If you can love all that ragged tribe, you will be a planet stronger than its surface shine.

I've never doubted the love my parents had for me when I was your age. I hope you'll never doubt our love for you. The treasure that is such a history has been one of the anchors of my existence, especially when I've felt the whole universe collapsing in on my self-pitying head. To be honest, when I was a boy, I sometimes felt ashamed of my parents and what they were doing, especially when my self-consciously tough friends were about. I know that at times you too feel embarrassed by and ashamed of us. Perhaps it's better if you consider your Dad as one large corny joke who loves you despite his flab and insensitivity towards you and your friends and our silk-black puppy cursed with the name 'The Midnight Vader'. I don't mind that at all. You see, I thrive on the enormous contradictions and absurdities that *are* our life. If there is a God, He must have a very courageous and fertile sense of humour, and an imagination that is an ocean of miracles.

On their children's birthdays, dutiful fathers are supposed to offer advice. I've always found it difficult to advise myself, let alone keep a straight face while advising others. So I won't foist my unoriginal platitudes on your golden head. (You don't accept advice too readily, anyway!) Except to say:

'Happy Birthday, Mele. I know the gods will continue to be kind to you, their blonde shaman.

'Men will continue to fall and bow at your feet. Don't treat them too cruelly, and don't demand they write poems for you or about you. Most of them will be too scared to. Or, like your father, won't have the gift of fishing love tunes out of their rib-cages.

'Don't give your generous heart to ungenerous black-eyed poets; they'll cut it to pieces and forget to sew the pieces together again, while they wander off in search of new tunes in other golden girls.

'Marry a millionaire who'll take loving care of your Dad in his miserable old age, providing him with the luxury and expensive squalor he has grown accustomed to. For that, your grateful Dad will write you as many poems – of any size, shape and sound – as you demand.'

Let this be the love poem I meant to write for you. If you think it doesn't measure up to the poems I've written for your sister and brother, then you can always say, 'At least he's written something specially for me'.

And perhaps you will then find in your beauty the strength to forgive me, and record in your diary: 'Today on my thirteenth birthday, Dad wrote me a love letter. He's been a word-merchant nearly all his life (he's forty-one years old – ancient, that is!) so he's very clever with words, but because this *is* my birthday – and he's paying for my birthday party – I want to believe (yes, I *do* believe) his declaration of love for me. And, dear Diary, my Dad *does* need my love; he's such a lousy poet!'

(By the way, don't forget to print AMEN after that.)

With all my alofa, Shalom! (That word means PEACE for 5% of our history, the word for the other 95% is WAR or TERROR!) *Dad.*

P.S. Your birthday party is going to cost me at least $100. That's a lot of alofa, kid! (You, in your usual clarity, are going to counter: 'Yes, but what's money got to do with the true alofa between father and daughter?')

So today the memory of my twenty-first birthday party has led me, once again, to my father and to a little more understanding of him and myself and, perhaps, to a forgiveness that should join fathers and sons during the last years of their lives together, that wise truce in the healing shadow of death. Out of that understanding has emerged more understanding of my own daughter, golden heir to her grandfather and a genealogy that reaches back to the gods in whom very few now believe, or know existed.

# Daughter of the Mango Season

'It's June 1894, and I'm fifty-five years old today,' Barker said to Mautu as they sat in cane chairs on the store veranda overlooking the malae. As usual, Peleiupu, Mautu's daughter, sat on the floor beside her father's chair. They were having a breakfast of strong tea and cabin bread. 'Fifty-five is old, isn't it?' Barker asked. Mautu nodded as he dunked his cabin bread in his mug of tea. 'Not many people here or in England live beyond forty,' Barker continued. 'I've been lucky. Haven't been seriously ill, ever . . .'

'Aren't you going to eat?' Mautu interrupted him.

Barker said, 'I'm not hungry.' Paused. 'How old are you?'

'Nearly forty-five.'

'The oldest man I've ever known was a Chinaman we took aboard in Hong Kong. About eighty he was. Small fist of a chap but very, very tough. Never said anything, not to me anyway. Bloody pagan he was. So you see, Mautu, we don't need to be Christians to live a long life.' Mautu, who was the village pastor, refused to take the bait. 'The next oldest was a Hindu. As black as midnight, and at seventy-something years old not a wrinkle on his face. Another heathen. In fact the longest-living people I've met were *not* Christians!' Mautu refused to reply. 'If old age is proof of the gods' blessings, then the pagan gods are more powerful.' He

134

paused dramatically and, gazing at Mautu from under lowered bushy eyebrows, added, 'Perhaps *your* God doesn't exist!'

'Going to be good mango season,' Mautu said in English as he gazed up at the mango trees that shaded the store. The high, sprawling trees were pink with blossoms and buds. Peleiupu wanted her father to offer their friend some consolation, an answer to grasp at. Mautu pushed away his food tray, looked at Barker and asked, 'Why is God's existence important to you if you not believe in Him?'

'It *isn't* important!'

'Then you not need to chase your own questions!' Mautu looked up at the mango trees again. 'Yes, the mangoes, they going to be a lot this season.'

'Why do you always talk in riddles?'

'It is you who deal in riddles!' Mautu replied. Barker looked away.

Peleiupu timed it perfectly. Just before Barker could jab his frustration at Mautu, she jumped up and picked up her father's food tray. She stood looking at Barker's tray.

'Yes, take mine too!' he said, finally.

'But you not eaten!' Mautu insisted.

'It isn't the food of this world that I need!'

'Not even sweet mangoes?' joked Mautu.

For the first time that morning, Barker relaxed and, looking up at the mango trees, said, 'Perhaps the sticky juice of the mango can hold my tattered fifty-five-year-old body together for a while longer!' When Peleiupu returned from the kitchen fale a few minutes later Barker said, 'Pele looks more like Lalaga than you.'

'Then she is not beautiful!' chuckled Mautu. Embarrassed, Pele avoided looking at them and sat down behind Mautu's chair.

'I wish my children were like Pele. The brats are total savages!'

Mautu reached out and touched the back of Barker's

right hand. 'All I know is you are a English Lord who is shipwrecked on a island full of sun and sky and mangoes and need nothing else!' Mautu said.

'Yes, I *am* the civilized English Lord shipwrecked in Paradise and I have no need of the Christian God, missionaries, other white-skinned Lords and crucifixes!' He laughed softly and clutched at Mautu's shoulder. 'I am a pagan in the midst of so much plenty! I am fifty-five years old today and I seek nothing and need nothing!'

'Perhaps just mangoes?' Mautu quipped.

'Yes, perhaps mangoes!'

As their laughter lost itself in the thick foliage of the mango trees, Peleiupu realized the two men had a profound need for each other, a bond so strong that one couldn't do without the other any more. They were so alike, this pagan papalagi trader and the Christian.

'Our annual Church Fono is to be held in two weeks time,' Mautu said in Samoan. 'Will you take us again in your fautasi?'

'Yes, but on one condition.'

'And what is that?'

'That you take Pele and Arona with you.' Barker winked at Peleiupu whose surprise was trapped breathlessly in her throat.

'Do you want to go?' Mautu asked her. Peleiupu nodded. 'You'd better ask your mother then!'

'We'll leave you and your party at Malua, and I'll take Pele and Arona into Apia.'

'I don't think so!'

'Don't you trust your papalagi pagan friend to care properly for your children?'

'It's not that,' mumbled Mautu. 'I don't like Apia.'

'Apia and the whole life that goes with it are here to stay, whether you like it or not. Your children will have to live with it.' He reached over and ruffled Peleiupu's hair. 'And Pele can cope with anything, even Apia!' he added. 'She watches and learns and understands quickly. Don't you, Pele?' Pele blushed. 'She is fortunate!'

Later as they walked away from Barker's store, Peleiupu glanced up at the mango trees. Their dark green foliage, now peppered pink and red with flowers, stirred lazily like slow spring water. She shivered with joy at the thought of visiting Apia.

'Do you like Barker?' Mautu asked. She nodded. 'Why?'

She pondered quickly and said, 'He is a very sad man, eh?'

'Barker *is* right about you: you *do* watch and learn and understand.'

They walked in silence the rest of the way.

'Mautu,' she pleaded as they walked up the back paepae of their fale, 'I want to go with Barker to Apia.'

'All right!' he whispered. Lalaga was weaving a mat in the centre of their fale. 'But you had better ask your mother about going on the trip.' Before she could insist on him asking Lalaga, he escaped to his desk at the other end of the fale.

'How is the papalagi gentleman?' Lalaga asked her in English. (Lalaga had taken to referring to Barker that way but there was no malice in it.)

'He is well,' Peleiupu replied formally, thus undermining Lalaga's line of attack. 'Let me do it.' She sat down. Lalaga slid away from the mat and let Peleiupu continue the weaving.

For a while they said nothing, and as Lalaga observed Peleiupu's deft hands and fingers weaving the mat she experienced a surge of pride in her daughter. At fourteen, Peleiupu was already an expert weaver of mats and highly skilled in other female crafts. Everything came easily to her, too easily, Lalaga had often thought. 'It is a gift from God!' Mautu had once allayed Lalaga's fears about Peleiupu. Even her English was now better than Mautu's. Yet Peleiupu always made herself appear less skilled than other people so as to make them feel more secure, safer, in her presence. For this, Lalaga loved her deeply, knowing that Peleiupu would not use her gift, her superior talents, to harm others.

'What did your father and the papalagi discuss this morning?' Lalaga asked, expecting Peleiupu, as usual, to check if anyone else was listening, before replying.

Peleiupu looked around the fale quickly and then said, 'Mautu says it's going to be a very good mango season this year.'

Lalaga wasn't going to be distracted *that* easily. 'What did the papalagi gentleman and your father, the prophet, talk about?'

Shrugging her shoulders, Peleiupu said, 'The usual.' Her hands worked more quickly.

Lalaga waited but got no further enlightenment, so she asked, 'And what is the usual?'

'The search for God.' Peleiupu's hands stopped their furious weaving. 'You believe in God, eh?' she asked.

'Of course I do!' Lalaga protested.

'That's what I thought.'

'You *thought* so!'

'Lalaga, some people don't believe in God,' Peleiupu explained.

Lalaga was frightened by what she felt she had to ask. 'Are you one of those people?'

Peleiupu's hands continued their nimble weaving. She said, 'Barker doesn't believe and I think many other papalagi are the same.'

'I knew that!' sighed Lalaga but, when she noticed the abrupt halt in Peleiupu's weaving, she tensed again, expecting another devastating revelation of heresy.

'Mautu believes, doesn't he?'

'How can you ask such a thing?' Lalaga was almost shouting. 'Your . . . your father is a Servant of God!'

Peleiupu ignored her anger and said, 'All I meant was that Mautu *sometimes* doubts.'

'Doubts what?' Lalaga insisted, angry with herself for allowing Peleiupu to question her belief.

'God,' was all Peleiupu said.

'Peleiupu!' Mautu called to her.

'Yes?'

'Get me a drink of water!'

Peleiupu scrambled up and out of the fale, leaving Lalaga grasping for meaning, like a fish kicking at the end of a line. She continued weaving but Peleiupu's revelation about Mautu's doubts kept picking at her.

Peleiupu was soon back with a mug of water for Mautu. While raising the drink to his mouth, Mautu whispered, 'What are you and your mother arguing about?'

'Nothing!' she whispered. Mautu started drinking. 'I just told her that you sometimes doubt the existence of God!' Mautu choked and coughed the water out in a splutter. 'That's true, isn't it?' she asked. He wiped his mouth with the back of his hand and, trying to steady his trembling hands, drank the rest of the water, slowly.

'Have you asked her about going to Upolu?' He handed her the empty tin mug.

She shook her head. 'Why don't you ask her?'

'It's best that you ask her,' he whispered. And before she could plead with him, he added, 'Go now, I've got a lot of work to do.' He continued writing.

She hesitated for a moment, turned swiftly, and hurried out of the fale.

'We haven't finished talking!' Lalaga stopped her.

Peleiupu went over reluctantly and sat down beside Lalaga, confused by her mother's unexpected anger and her father's timidity and refusal to get permission for her and Arona to go to Apia. Everything was straightforward, but adults, especially parents, made things complicated, stupidly unreasonable, she thought. She was only fourteen years old, yet she had to be ever so patient with their lack of understanding, their slow decision-making, and the eternal complications they made of their lives (and everyone else's!). Most of them were so *unwise*, yes, that was her description.

'Going to be a good mango season,' she remarked. She tried to dispel her confusion with the thought of fat, delicious, succulent mangoes, but couldn't. Beside her, Lalaga's presence was a solid rock pillar. She wasn't going to offer to do the weaving any more. 'Where are Arona and the other children?' she asked.

'I don't know!' Lalaga replied. She suddenly realized her daughter no longer referred to herself as a child, and it wasn't out of any pretence or arrogance. Peleiupu simply did not think of herself as a child. And, physically, she was quickly blossoming into a woman, tall and supple. Peleiupu wasn't self-conscious about this physical transformation either. It was as if, anticipating well beforehand every change in her life, she adjusted to it before it occurred.

'Very hot, eh?' Peleiupu commented, noticing the beads of sweat slithering down her mother's arms and face. 'Where's everybody gone?' All the neighbouring fale appeared empty of people.

'Working in their plantations or fishing, you know that!'

'Yes,' sighed Peleiupu, 'but where are Arona and Ruta and Naomi and the other children of our aiga?'

'Swimming, probably. Now stop your questions! Here, you weave!'

When Lalaga looked out of the fale and saw that their mango trees beside the road were covered with blossoms, she heard herself saying, 'Yes, it is going to be a rich mango harvest.'

'Mautu was the first to observe that this morning.' Peleiupu paused in her work and, gazing steadily at Lalaga, said, 'Funny how you can make an important observation the property of everyone by just pointing it out to someone else who then points it out to someone else and so on. Of course it has to be an observation that is important to those other people. Like the other morning, while Arona and I and the other children were in our plantation collecting coconuts, I suddenly *heard* the silence in all that growth . . .'

'Heard it?'

'Yes, I heard the silence – it was deep and still, a huge kind presence all around us and in us . . . And when I heard it, I told Arona to stand still, silently, and listen to it. He did. I told him to shut his eyes. He did. Then I asked him if he was hearing it. He nodded. Then we asked the others in turn to listen. And when we had all had a turn, we all closed our eyes together and listened as a group. And we all heard it and allowed it to become part of us.'

'What did you think that particular silence was?' Lalaga pressed her, knowing that Peleiupu, as usual, had glimpsed a deeper meaning to it.

'It was the land itself,' she explained. 'The silence of these islands. It must have been here when God created our country. And has always been here.'

'But why is it important?'

'I don't know yet how to explain it,' she said. 'Perhaps it is important because if we refuse to hear it, or let it be part of us, we will become other creatures . . . I don't know. Arona knows better. He doesn't allow his thinking to get in the way. *He just knows*. He lets things become what they are in himself.' She paused and added, 'It is bad to think too much, Barker keeps telling Mautu. He is right . . .'

'But Barker does nothing else but chase his thoughts round and round!' laughed Lalaga. 'That's why he can't believe in anything!'

'That's the palagi way, that's how palagi people are.'

'And your father?'

Aware that Lalaga had once again led her deftly to a discussion she wanted to avoid, Peleiupu said, 'May I go for a swim?' Before Lalaga could pin her down again, Peleiupu called, 'Mautu, may I go for a swim?'

'All right!' he replied.

141

And Peleiupu was out of the fale and running towards the pool.

Lalaga continued to weave her mat, refusing to ask Mautu directly about his doubts because he was, like Peleiupu, very adept at dodging her questions.

It was almost midday and the sun was snared in a smother of thick cloud that seemed to have oozed out of the sky's belly. Only the quick, soft squeaking and scratching of Lalaga's fingers against the pandanus strands disturbed the quiet. Occasionally, she heard Mautu shift in his wooden chair. Mangoes, she thought inadvertently, and then cursed herself for having thought that. Why did her daughter understand more than she? She had no right to, she was only a child!

On their way home from the pool, Peleiupu edged up to Arona and whispered, 'Do you want to visit Upolu?' Arona looked straight ahead. A brother, at his age, should no longer be seen displaying affection for his sister. 'Barker and Mautu will take us if we want to go.'

'Who said?' Arona asked.

'Not too loud!' she whispered. Ruta and Naomi and the others were too busy talking among themselves to hear anyway. 'Mautu and Lalaga and the elders are attending the Church Fono at Malua. Do you want to go?' He nodded once, sternly. 'Lalaga hasn't said we can go though,' she added, hoping he would volunteer to persuade Lalaga. He said nothing. 'Did you hear?' He nodded once. 'Well?' she asked.

'Well what?'

'We won't be able to go if Lalaga says no!'

'You ask her then,' was his curt reply. He looked so aloof and bulky in the noon sun, with the droplets of water glistening, like fish scales, in his hair and over his body, that she hesitated from persuading him any further.

'You're her favourite,' she ventured onto precarious ground.

142

'I'll ask Lalaga!' Ruta volunteered.

'Ask her what?' Peleiupu snapped.

'Whatever you want me to!'

'It is not your concern!' Arona stressed, just like their father when he wanted quiet. Ruta shrugged her shoulders and resumed her whispered conversation with her friends.

They noticed that some of the older girls and boys were gathering in the fale classrooms behind their main fale for their afternoon lessons. Lalaga was still weaving.

'I'll ask her,' Arona said, finally, and then walked away from her.

As usual, after lotu and their evening meal, Mautu conducted an English lesson with Lalaga, his children and the brightest Satoa children. During these lessons, whenever Mautu didn't know the meanings of words or their correct pronunciation, he got Peleiupu to explain them. However, he always re-checked with Barker later. Sometimes when Mautu couldn't take the class, Peleiupu took it; and secretly, Lalaga and the others preferred her relaxed, democratic, patient style of teaching. Mautu also gave her all the students' assignments and exercises to mark.

After the lesson that night, Peleiupu and the other girls strung up the mosquito nets and soon all the children were in the nets and falling asleep. Instead of sitting up with her parents, Peleiupu got into the net where she slept with Ruta and Naomi and three other girls, pulled her sheet up to her chin, and pretended to be sleeping. Intermittently, however, she would peer through her half-closed eyelids at her parents and Arona who were playing cards beside the lamp a few paces away, hoping to hear Lalaga's decision about their going to Upolu.

Like the sudden pulling back of a curtain, she was awake. It was bright morning and the other children were outside picking up the fallen leaves. She rolled

143

out, untied the net quickly and folded it with her sleeping-sheet and placed it on the lowest rafter, with the sleeping-mats.

Arona and three of his friends were behind the kitchen fale scraping coconuts to feed the chickens, but because there were no girls with them she couldn't go and ask him.

At the drums of rain-water under the breadfruit trees, she filled a basin, washed her face and combed her hair, all the time keeping an eye on her brother.

As she helped the other girls in the kitchen fale cook their morning meal, she tried not to think of Lalaga's decision. Shortly, when she saw Arona strolling through the scatter of banana trees towards the beach, she got up and pretended to be heading for the lavatory that was located at the edge of the beach behind a thick stand of palm trees.

'What did she say?' she called to him. He was standing up to his thighs in the sea, his back to her, washing a coconut strainer he had brought with him. He continued as if he hadn't heard her. She moved up to the water's edge. 'What did Lalaga say?' she repeated. Raising the strainer with both hands, Arona squeezed it in one long drawn-out action, and the water dribbled through his hands like solid white smoke and splattered into the surface of the sea.

He waded back towards the beach. 'She will decide by tomorrow.'

'Tomorrow?' she cried, stamping her right foot into the thickly wet sand. He nodded and started to walk past her. 'But why?'

'Don't worry, she'll let us go!'

'She had better!' she snapped.

There was no one else in the main fale as she sat with Arona facing Lalaga who, she sensed, was avoiding looking at her. In the pit of her belly a ferocious beast was inflating itself, threatening to fill every nook and cranny of her shape. She could hardly breathe; sobs were breaking from her chest like huge bubbles about to burst but she swallowed them down repeatedly.

'. . . Arona may come with us,' Lalaga was saying, 'but you'll have to stay and run our classes . . .'

' 'I won't. No!' The choking cry broke from her mouth. She slapped at her knees, and she was sobbing.

'Don't you talk to me like that!' ordered Lalaga. 'No child talks to her mother like that. You hear me!'

'I want to go!' Peleiupu cried. She sprang up, fists clenched at her sides, her huge tears dripping down to the mat. 'I'm going!'

'I won't allow any child of mine to talk to me like that. Hear me?' Lalaga re-hitched her lavalava. 'If you don't watch out, I'll beat you!'

Peleiupu scuttled across the fale. At the front threshold, she wheeled, wiped her face fiercely with her hands, and called, 'I'm going and you can't stop me!'

'Get me the broom!' Lalaga ordered Arona.

Peleiupu jumped down on to the grass and started running furiously across the malae.

'You wait!' Lalaga threatened. 'You wait until I get you tonight!'

They watched Peleiupu disappearing into a stand of bananas and into the plantations. 'Go and bring her back, now!' Lalaga ordered Arona who rose slowly, glanced at her, and started ambling out of the fale. 'And hurry up!' she chased him.

For a while, Lalaga stood on the front paepae gazing after her children, then when she realized the neighbours were watching her, she retreated to her weaving.

'I'll show her,' she kept repeating. 'She thinks she knows more than her own mother – the animal! Just wait. I've spent my life slaving for her. Just wait!'

A short while later, however, when she remembered how determined her daughter was, she visualized, with increasing panic, Peleiupu in a fragile canoe paddling suicidally across the hungry straits which would inevitably swallow her up. Then more frightening still, she

saw Peleiupu up in a tree fixing a noose round her neck.
She scrambled up and out into the classrooms where
she instructed the oldest students to follow Arona and
search for Peleiupu.

The undergrowth was a dense green sea sucking her
into its depths as she ran, her feet making plopping,
sucking sounds in the muddy track. 'I'll show her! I'll
show her!' Peleiupu repeated. Ahead, the ifi tree was a
massive mother with arms outstretched to welcome her.

She jumped up, clung to the lowest branch, kicked
up and landed on the next branch, then, branch by
branch, she climbed until she reached a platform of
interlocking branches, lay down on her back and cried
up into the maze of leaves and branches and thin rays
of light.

This was 'her tree', her refuge whenever she was
troubled. When she had first discovered it five years
previously it had intimidated her with its heavy brooding presence; an octopus, she had thought. Its rich,
fertile smell of mould had made her think of supernatural beasts. However, one morning after a nasty
argument with Arona and Lalaga, she had found
herself up in the ifi's protective shade, and, as she had
lain on the platform, the tree's breathing and aromatic
odour had healed her hurt. Soon after that, she had
heard Filivai, the Satoa taulasea, say that certain trees,
in pre-Christian times, had been the homes of aitu
and atua. After fifty years of missionary conversion,
aitu had become evil beings to be feared, and there was
only one Atua. Her ifi tree had an aitu, she came to
believe after hours of relaxing in its green healing. Her
tree was also part of Nature, a spiritual force she kept
reading about in English books. She wondered what
ancient aitu lived in her tree, and in her imagination
tried to give form to that aitu. She tried her mother,
then the taulasea Filivai, then a combination of all the
women she admired. One day she even pictured her

tree's aitu as one of Snow White's dwarfs; she tried the supernatural beings she had read about in Barker's books – the Cyclops, the Genii, Unicorn. None of them fitted, she decided. So she tried all the animals she knew. Then all the fish and other sea creatures. Her patient search was methodical and led her deeper into the rich depths of the garden of her imagination. Years later, especially in moments of crisis, she would realize that in her search for her tree's aitu she had explored and groped her way towards the wisdom of her imagination, to a faith that lay beyond logic and belief.

One overcast afternoon as she sat cross-legged on the platform, hands on her knees, her back straight, gazing motionlessly into the foliage, she let her thoughts settle into a still pool, so still a whisper could shatter it. She waited. She thought she was dreaming: she saw herself sitting cross-legged on the platform. She waited. Gradually, almost as if a slow melting was radiating through her pores into all the corners of her being, she inhaled the tangy aroma of the moss that covered, like a cloak, the bark of her tree. She relaxed, with an ecstatic sigh, and the odour not only filled her but the sky and bush and all the creatures in it. Everything was drunk with it, and she *knew* that the presence of the moss's odour was the aitu of her tree, and it was in her soul now.

When she surfaced from the spell, evening was starting to cover her tree like a silk black garment.

A few days later, when she began to doubt her faith in her aitu, she wandered to Filivai's home and played a game of lape with the children of Filivai's aiga. Halfway through the boisterous game, she pretended she had taken ill and went into Filivai's fale.

Filivai was using a stone pestle to pound a mixture of leaves and coconut oil. The pungent odour of the potion reminded Peleiupu of her tree's aitu, as she sat down a few paces opposite Filivai. Because she was thought of by the Satoans as 'Mautu's very gifted daughter', she was welcomed in all their homes at any time. However, like almost all Satoans she was wary of Filivai because she was a healer not only of physical ailments but of ma'i aitu. Filivai's powers, she heard Satoans whisper, came from the Days of the Darkness: Filivai was heir to an evil heritage which the missionaries and pastors had exorcized (and were still exorcizing). But, unlike other taulasea Peleiupu had heard about, Filivai was an earnest Christian who refused to heal ma'i aitu, unless it was absolutely necessary. And, before performing such healing, she always asked Mautu, her pastor, for permission to do so. Her father, Peleiupu remembered, had never refused Filivai, and she wondered why. Later in her life Peleiupu would observe that her people's belief in the Christian Atua, the Holy Spirit, was only the top third of the pyramid which included, in its three-dimensional body and belly, a feared assembly of savage aitu, sauali'i, sau'ai, and the papalagi-introduced ghosts, vampires, frankensteins, demons, devils and Satan. Linked to this observation was the perception that all living creatures were part of a world inhabited by other beings who were both visible and invisible, benevolent and destructive. Now that they were Christians, the Satoans tried not to discuss, within Mautu's hearing, these other beings. From what Peleiupu heard and observed, she knew that many Satoans, especially the elders, sometimes met and talked with the spirits of their ancestors. At times they even suffered the wrath of those spirits, and were sometimes possessed by them. Even her parents, who professed unshakable faith in reason and the Bible, were not free of the feared menagerie which inhabited the murky depths of the pyramid. To her death Lalaga would deny, verbally, the existence of the menagerie, but Peleiupu knew Lalaga feared its existence. On the other hand her father, whose ancestors had been taula aitu, would come to believe more profoundly and without fear in what he called 'that other reality' in which dwelled the banished spirits of his taula aitu ancestors and their atua Fatutapu and all the other presences and spirits. Mautu would never reveal this to his congregation, but Peleiupu would love him more abundantly for it.

'How is your father?' Filivai greeted her.

'He is well, thank you.'

'And your mother?'

'She is well too, thank you.'

Filivai trickled more coconut oil into the potion and continued pounding it. Peleiupu watched her. Filivai was over sixty, one of the oldest Satoans, but she looked as young as Lalaga. Only the network of wrinkles on her forehead and cheeks and the looseness of her flesh betrayed her age. Her pendulous breasts, blue-veined around the almost black nipples, hung down to her belly and shook in rhythm to her pounding. She wore a stained lavalava and a tiputa draped over her shoulders.

'It's going to be a good mango season,' Peleiupu heard herself saying.

'If it rains heavily while the mangoes are in flower, there won't be many mangoes.'

'Why not?'

'The rain will break many of the flowers,' Filivai said. Peleiupu wanted more details but wasn't going to be impolite. 'Is it true you read a lot of books?' Filivai asked.

'Not as much as my father or Barker,' she admitted. Then, quickly perceiving the opening, added, 'Do you like Barker?'

'He's married to a woman of my aiga,' Filivai evaded her.

'He doesn't go to church or believe in God, eh?' Peleiupu sensed Filivai wasn't surprised by that.

'You didn't come to talk about the papalagi, eh?' Filivai's unexpected parry surprised Peleiupu who, for a pause, didn't know how to counter. 'I'll wipe my hands, then we'll talk.' Using a corner of her lavalava, Filivai started wiping her hands clean of the sticky bits of leaves and oil. 'How many years are you now?'

'Fourteen.'

'But your mind is older!' Filivai remarked. Peleiupu wondered how Filivai had lost her two top middle teeth; there was a thin, white perpendicular scar on her upper lip, also. 'Your brain is much older.'

Flattery always embarrassed Peleiupu, so she said, 'I must go!'

'Don't go! I am glad you came to talk with me.'

A short while later they were conversing easily.

'I have a tree,' Peleiupu said.

'What kind of tree?'

'A ifi. I remember you telling my parents that in the olden days some trees had aitu or atua.' Peleiupu paused. Filivai nodded. 'My tree has one.'

'Have you told your parents that?' Filivai asked as if Peleiupu's revelation wasn't unusual. Peleiupu shook her head. 'You shouldn't let them know: they are God's servants and may not understand.'

'That is why I came to you.' No reaction from Filivai. 'The atua in my tree reveals itself to me through the odour of the tree. Is that possible?' Filivai nodded. 'It is a kind atua; it heals my pain, always.'

'It comes easily, doesn't it?' Filivai asked. Peleiupu didn't comprehend. 'You know, you see without knowing how you do it. It is a great gift,' Filivai said. 'From God,' she added hurriedly. 'Because of it most people will be frightened of you. Do your parents know about it?'

'If you mean I have intelligence, then my parents know I have it, especially my mother.'

'Is she happy about it?'

Peleiupu pondered for a moment, and then admitted, 'Don't think so!'

'What about your father?'

'He knows, but he is too busy with his books.'

'I knew a young girl once. She had the gift too,' Filivai said more to herself than Peleiupu.

'Were other people wary of her?'

'Yes,' Filivai emphasized. 'Yes, very frightened when they discovered she could see into the world of atua and aitu and other presences. A world outlawed by the Church . . .'

'What happened to her?' Peleiupu asked. She thought she could see tears in Filivai's eyes.

'She is alive. She is a simple healer,' Filivai said.

'And the gift?'

Filivai looked away. 'I must continue with my work.'

'I will go now,' Peleiupu said, rising reluctantly to her feet.

'You must learn to hide the gift,' Filivai said. Peleiupu glanced back at her. 'Don't ever try to destroy it. Or betray it. It is what you are.'

'May I come and see you again – if I need to?'

Filivai nodded once. 'I don't have the courage and may not be able to help you.'

'Thank you. I'll go now.'

'Don't expect too much from me!' Filivai pleaded.

Peleiupu walked out onto the malae where the scramble of children was still playing lape.

'Pele's in our team!' one of her friends called.

Peleiupu looked back at Filivai and found her gazing at her. Peleiupu waved once. Filivai nodded. Quickly Peleiupu decided what she had to do to survive, and skipped into the noisy game of lape, laughing and joking, a girl who appeared to be totally absorbed in the game.

The sun was setting. Two of the search groups had returned only to be instructed by a now panicking Lalaga to continue the search. (Mautu was due home from his fishing trip with Barker, and Lalaga didn't want to face his wrath.) Some of the old women came and consoled her. They sat on the paepae, looking hopefully up the bush and hills and mountain range that darkened, like a fierce tidal wave, as evening dropped. 'She's too smart, she thinks she knows every-

thing!' Lalaga kept saying. 'She's rebellious, disobedient, difficult!' They nodded in sympathy but didn't
believe Peleiupu was like that.

Unexpectedly Lalaga saw Mautu by the kitchen fale,
pulling his bush-knife out of the thatching. She hurried
towards him.

'I know already!' he called to her. In his command,
she sensed an enormous anger. She stopped. He
marched past her.

She watched until he was at a safe distance heading
for Barker's home. 'That's why she's like that!' she called
after him. 'You always side with her!'

For a while, as the cicadas cried around her, she wept,
more out of fear than anger, then she wiped away her
tears, and returned and sat with the other women in the
main fale, and waited for Mautu and Barker and the
search parties to return.

'Mautu and Barker told us to come home,' Arona
informed Lalaga and the elders. They had their lotu, the
young people served the elders (the old men and women
of Satoa who hadn't gone on the search) their evening
meal, which they ate in strained silence, with everyone
trying not to see the fear in Lalaga; then the young
people ate, bathed, got into their nets and fell asleep
easily, exhausted from tracking through the plantations
and the bush.

Most of the elders tried to stay awake with Lalaga but
fell asleep one by one as the night progressed. Beside
the centre lamp, Lalaga kept her vigil. At times, she
prayed for forgiveness, asking God to save her daughter
whom she had mistreated. Every time she dared look
into the darkness outside, unwelcome images of a
dead Peleiupu jumped into her mind and she would
shut her eyes and pray more fervently.

The rooster's crowing unclenched the centre of her
head it seemed, and forced her out of her sleep. She
was still sitting beside the lamp; the elders, wrapped
tightly in their sleeping-sheets, lay in rows around her;

someone was snoring like a boiling kettle. Dawn was spilling out of the east and splashing across the sky. No Mautu. No Peleiupu. The raw touch of panic caught at her throat. She held back the cry. She staggered up, gripped by the most overwhelming sense of helplessness she had ever experienced. Her daughter, how she loved her!

There were people washing themselves at the drums of rain-water beside the kitchen fale. In the half-light she saw Mautu and Barker among them. Her feet started running, dragging her with them, towards Mautu before she could stop them, and she watched them melt their quick prints in the dew-covered ground.

Mautu turned his back slowly, surely, towards her, dismissing her. She stopped. She looked at the other men. They looked away.

Barker stepped in front of her. 'Peleiupu is all right,' he said in Samoan. 'She sleeping with her sisters . . .' Lalaga blocked her mouth with her hands, wheeled and started hurrying back to the main fale. 'She came back on her own. We find her in the net when we return this morning!' Barker called.

She was ripping up the side of the mosquito net and reaching down at Peleiupu. *'Don't you touch my daughter!'* Mautu's command stopped her. No one moved. Not a sound. As though Mautu's order had stilled everything. She again tried to push her angry outstretched hands down towards the sleeping Peleiupu. 'Don't!' Mautu's threat was final. She dared not disobey. 'Let my daughter sleep!'

Lalaga stumbled past him towards the beach. Mautu got a towel and, with Barker and the other men, headed for the pool. Once they were out of sight, the elders and the children dispersed to their homes, unwilling to face their pastor's anger.

Ruta and Naomi and the other children made little noise as they put away the mosquito nets and sleeping-mats and then went to the kitchen fale, leaving the spacious main fale to Peleiupu who was sleeping peacefully in the large net that was shivering, like a live white creature, in the soft breeze.

No one, not even Arona, would dare mention anything to Peleiupu about her rebellion. Not ever. They all sensed that Mautu wanted it that way.

They also assumed, without asking Mautu or Lalaga, that Peleiupu and Arona would accompany the elders and Barker to the Malua Fono and Apia.

But from that morning on, they noticed that whenever Peleiupu needed to be chastised or disciplined – a rare occurrence – Lalaga left it to Mautu. 'After all, she is *his* daughter!' Lalaga told the Satoans.

# Crocodile

Miss Susan Sharon Willersey, known to all her students as Crocodile Willersey, was our House Mistress for the five years I was at boarding school. I recall, from reading a brief history of our school, that she had been born in 1908 in a small Waikato farming town and, at the age of ten, had enrolled at our Preparatory School, had then survived (brilliantly) our high school, had attended university and graduated MA (Honours in Latin), and had returned to our school to teach and be a dormitory mistress, and, a few years later, was put in charge of Beyle House, our House.

So when I started in 1953, Crocodile was in her fit mid-forties, already a school institution more myth than bone, more goddess than human (and she tended to behave that way!).

Certain stories, concerning the derivation of her illustrious nickname, prevailed (and were added to) during my time at school.

One story, in line with the motto of our school (which is: Perseverance is the Way to Knowledge), had it that Miss Willersey's first students called her Crocodile because she was a model of perseverance and fortitude, which they believed were the moral virtues of a crocodile.

Another story claimed that because Miss Willersey was a devout Anglican, possessing spiritual purity beyond blemish (is that correct?), an Anglican missionary, who had visited our school after spending twenty invigorating years in the Dark Continent (his description), had described Miss Willersey in our school assembly as a saint with the courage and purity and powers of the African crocodile (which was sacred to many tribes). Proof of her steadfastness and purity, so this story went, was her kind refusal to marry the widowed missionary because, as she reasoned (and he was extremely understanding), she was already married to her church, to her school and students, and to her profession.

The most unkindly story attributed her nickname to her appearance: Miss Willersey looked and behaved like a crocodile – she was long, long-teethed, long-eared, long-fingered, long-arsed, long-everythinged. Others also argued she had skin like crocodile hide, and that her behaviour was slippery, always spyful, decisively cruel and sadistic and unforgiving, like a crocodile's.

As a new third-former and a naive Samoan who had been reared to obey her elders without question, I refused to believe the unfavourable stories about Miss Willersey's nickname. Miss Willersey was always kind and helpful (though distant, as was her manner with all of us) to me in our House and during her Latin classes. (Because I was in the top third form I *had* to take Latin though I was really struggling with another foreign language, English, and New Zealand English at that!) We felt (and liked it) that she was also treating all her 'Island girls' (there were six of us) in a specially protective way. 'You must always be proud of your race!' she kept reminding us. (She made it a point to slow down her English when speaking to us so we could understand her.)

During her Latin classes, I didn't suffer her verbal and physical (the swift ruler) chastisements, though I was a dumb, bumbling student. Not for ten months anyway.

However, in November during that magical third-form year, I *had* to accept the negative interpretations of Miss Willersey's nickname.

I can't remember what aspect of Latin we were

revising orally in class that summer day. All I remember well were: Croc's mounting anger as student after student (even her brightest) kept making errors; my loudly beating heart as her questioning came closer and closer to me; the stale smell of cardigans and shoes; Croc's long physique stretching longer, more threateningly; and some of my classmates snivelling into their handkerchiefs as Croc lacerated them verbally for errors (sins) committed.

'Life!' she called coldly, gazing at her feet. Silence. I didn't realize she was calling me. (My name is Olamai-ileoti Monroe. Everyone at school called me Ola and *translated* it as Life which became my nickname.) 'Life!' she repeated, this time her blazing eyes were boring into me. (I was almost wetting my pants, and this was contrary to Miss Willersey's constant exhortation to us: ladies learn early how to control their bladders!)

I wanted desperately to say, 'Yes, Miss Willersey?' but I found I couldn't, I was too scared.

'Life?' She was now advancing towards me, filling me with her frightening lengthening. 'You *are* called Life, aren't you, Monroe? That *is* your nickname?'

Nodding my head, I muttered, 'Yes – yes!' A squeaking. My heart was struggling like a trapped bird in my throat. 'Yes, yes, Miss Willersey!'

'And your name is Life, isn't it?'

'Yes!' I was almost in tears. (Leaking everywhere I was!)

'What does Ola mean exactly?'

'Life, Miss Willersey.'

'But Ola is not a noun, is it?' she asked.

Utterly confused, leaking every which way, and thoroughly shit-scared, I just shook my head furiously.

'Ola doesn't mean Life, it is a verb, it means "to live", "to grow", doesn't it?' I nodded furiously.

'Don't you know even your own language, young lady?' I bowed my head (in shame); my trembling hands were clutching the desk-top. 'Speak up, young lady!'

'No, Miss Willersey!' I swallowed back my tears.

'Now, Miss Life, or, should I say, Miss To-Live, let's see if you know Latin a little better than you know your own language!' Measuredly, she marched back to the front of our class. Shit, shit, shit! I cursed myself (and my fear) silently. Her footsteps stopped. Silence. She was turning to face me. Save me, someone!

'Excuse me, Miss Willersey?' the saving voice intruded.

'Yes, what is it?'

'I think I heard someone knocking on the door, Miss Willersey.' It was Gill, the ever-aware, always courageous Gill. The room sighed. Miss Willersey had lost the initiative. 'Shall I go and see who it is, Miss Willersey?' Gill asked, standing up and gazing unwaveringly at Miss Willersey. We all focused our eyes on her too. A collective defiance and courage. For a faltering moment I thought she wasn't going to give in.

Then she looked away from Gill and said, 'Well, all right and be quick about it!'

'You all right, Miss To-Live?' Gill asked me after class when all my friends crowded round me in the corridor.

'Yes!' I thanked her.

'Croc's a bloody bitch!' someone said.

'Yeah!' the others echoed.

So for the remainder of my third-form year and most of my fourth year I *looked* on Miss Susan Sharon Willersey as the Crocodile to be wary of, to pretend good behaviour with, to watch all the time in case she struck out at me. Not that she ever again treated me unreasonably in class despite my getting dumber and dumber in Latin (and less and less afraid of her).

In those two years, Gill topped our class in Latin, with little effort and in courageously clever defiance of Crocodile. Gill also helped me get the magical 50% I needed to pass and stay out of Crocodile's wrath.

\*

Winter was almost over, the days were getting warmer, our swimming pool was filled and the more adventurous (foolhardy?) used it regularly. Gill and I (and the rest of Miss Rashly's cross-country team) began to rise before light and run the four miles through the school farm. Some mornings, on our sweaty way back, we would meet a silent Crocodile in grey woollen skirt and thick sweater and boots, striding briskly through the cold.

'Morning, girls!' she would greet us.

'Morning, Miss Willersey!' we would reply.

'Exercise, regular exercise, that's the way, girls!'

In our fourth-form dormitory, my bed was nearest the main door that opened out to the lounge opposite which was the front door to Crocodile's apartment, forbidden domain unless we were summoned to it to be questioned (and punished) for a misdemeanour, or invited to it for hot cocoa and biscuits (prefects were the usual invitees!). Because it *was* forbidden territory we were curious about what went on in there: how Croc lived, what she looked like without her formidably thick make-up and stern outfits, and so on. As a Samoan I wasn't familiar with how papalagi (and especially Crocodile) lived out their private lives. I tried but I couldn't picture Miss Willersey in her apartment in her bed or in her bath in nothing else (not even in her skin) but in her make-up, immaculately coiffured hair and severe suits. (I couldn't even imagine her using the toilet! Pardon the indiscretion which is unbecoming of one of Miss Willersey's girls!)

The self-styled realists and sophisticates among us – and they were mainly seniors who had to pretend to such status – whispered involved and terribly upsetting (exciting) tales about Crocodile's men (and lack of men), who visited (and didn't visit) her in the dead of night. We, the gullible juniors, inexperienced in the ways of men and sex, found these lurid tales erotically exciting (upsetting) but never admitted publicly we *were* excited.

We all feigned disgust and disbelief. And quite frankly I couldn't imagine Miss Willersey (in her virgin skin) with a man (in his experienced skin) in her bed in the wildly lustful embrace of *knowing each other* (our Methodist Bible-class teacher's description of the act of fucking!). No, I really tried, but couldn't put Crocodile into that forbidden but feverishly exciting position. At the time I *did* believe in Miss Willersey's strict moral standards concerning the relationship between the sexes. (I was a virgin, and that's what Miss Willersey and my other elders wanted me to retain and give to the man I married.)

One sophisticate, the precociously pretentious and overweight daughter of a Wellington surgeon and one of Crocodile's pet prefects, suggested that Croc's nightly visitors *weren't* men. That immediately put more disgustingly exciting possibilities into our wantonly frustrated (and virgin) imaginations.

'Who then?' an innocent junior asked.

'What then?' another junior asked.

'Impossible. Bloody filthy!' the wise Gill countered.

'It happens!' the fat sophisticate argued.

'How do you know?' someone asked.

'I just know, that's all!'

'Because your mother is a lesbian!' Gill, the honest, socked it to her. We had to break up the fight between Gill and the Wellington sophisticate.

'Bugger her!' Gill swore as we led her out of the locker room. 'She sucks up to Miss Willersey and then says Croc's a les!'

'What's – what's a les . . . lesbian?' I forced myself to ask Gill at prep that evening. She looked surprised, concluded with a shrug that I didn't really know, printed something on a piece of paper and, after handing it to me, watched me read it.

A FEMALE WHO IS ATTRACTED TO OTHER FEMALES!!!

'What do you mean?' I whispered. (We weren't allowed to talk during prep.)

She wrote on the paper: *'You Islanders are supposed to know a lot more about sex than us poor pakehas. A les is a female who does it with other females. Savvy?'*

*'Up you too!'* I wrote back. We started giggling.

'Gill, stand up!' the prefect on duty called.

'Oh, shit!' Gill whispered under her breath.

'Were you talking?'

'Life just wanted me to spell a word for her!' Gill replied.

'What word?'

'Les –', Gill started to say. My heart nearly stopped. 'Life wanted to know how to spell "lesson"!' Relief.

'Well, spell it out aloud for all of us!' And Gill did so, crisply, all the time behind her back giving the prefect the up-you sign.

After this incident, I noticed myself observing the Crocodile's domain more closely for unusual sounds, voices, visitors, and, though I refused to think of the possibility of her being a lesbian, I tried to discern a pattern in her female visitors (students included), but no pattern emerged. Also, there were no unusual sounds. (Croc didn't even sing in the bath!)

Some creature, almost human, was trapped in the centre of my head, sobbing pitifully, mourning an enormous loss. It was wrapping its pain around my dreaming and I struggled to break away from its tentacles. I couldn't. I woke to find myself awake (and relieved I wasn't strangling in the weeping) in the dark of our dormitory. Everyone else was fast asleep.

Then I knew it was Miss Willersey. I knew it and tried not to panic, not give in to the feeling I wasn't going to be able to cope. I wrapped the blankets round my head. It was none of my business! But I couldn't escape.

I found myself standing with my ear to Miss Willersey's door. Shivering. Her light was on, I could tell from the slit of light under the door. The sobbing was more audible but it sounded muffled, as if she was crying into a pillow or cushion. Uncontrolled. Emerging from the depths of a fathomless grief. Drawing me into its depths.

My hand opened the door before I could stop it. Warily I peered into the blinding light. My eyes adjusted quickly to the glare. The neat and orderly arrangement of furniture, wall pictures, ornaments, and bookcases came into focus. Miss Willersey was enthroned in an armchair against the far wall, unaware of my presence, unaware of where she was and who she was, having relinquished in her grief all that was the Crocodile. She was dressed in a shabby dressing-gown, brown slippers, hair in wild disarray, tears melting away her thick make-up in streaks down her face, her long-fingered hands clasped to her mouth trying to block back the sound.

Shutting the door behind me quietly, I edged closer to her, hoping she would see me and order me out of her room and then I wouldn't have to cope with the new, fragile, vulnerable Miss Willersey. I didn't want to.

All around us (and in me) her grief was like the incessant buzzing of a swarm of bees, around and around, spiralling up out of the hollow hive of her being and weaving round and round in my head, driving me towards her and her sorrow which had gone beyond her courage to measure and bear.

And I moved into her measure and, lost for whatever else to do, wrapped my arms around her head, and immediately her arms were around me tightly and my body was the cushion for her grief.

At once she became my comfort, the mother I'd never had but had always yearned for, and I cried silently into her pain. Mother and daughter, daughter and mother. A revelation I hoped would hold true for as long as I was to know her.

Her weeping eased. Her arms relaxed around me. She turned her face away. 'Please!' she murmured. I looked away. Got the box of tissues on the table and put it in her shaking hands. I looked away. Tearing out a handful of tissues, she wiped her eyes and face.

I started to leave. 'It is Ola, isn't it?' she asked, face still turned away. In her voice was a gentleness I had never heard in it before.

'Yes.'

'Thank you. I'm . . . I'm sorry you've had to see me like this.' She was ripping out more tissues.

'Is there anything else I can do?' I asked.

'No, thank you.' She started straightening her dressing-gown and hair. The Crocodile was returning. I walked to the door. 'Ola!' she stopped me. I didn't look back at her. 'This is our secret. Please don't tell the others?'

'I won't, Miss Willersey. Good-night!'

'Good-night, Ola!'

I shut the door behind me, quietly, and on *our* secret.

Next morning there was a short article in the newspaper about her mother's death in Hamilton, in an old people's home. Miss Willersey left on the bus for Hamilton that afternoon.

'The Croc's mother's crocked!' some girls joked at our table at dinner that evening.

Yes, Crocodile Willersey remained married to her school and students until she died in 1982. By becoming a school tradition and a mythical being in the memories of all her students (generations of them) she has lived on, and we will bequeath her to our children.

Miss Susan Sharon Willersey, the Crocodile, I will always think of you with genuine alofa. (And forgive me – I've forgotten nearly all the Latin you taught me!) By the way, you were wrong about the meaning of Ola; it can also be a noun, Life.

# Hamlet

*(for Jo Nacola)*

---

Most of us (unfortunately) never discover the passions, obsessions and talents which we possess. The fortunate (among us) sometimes discover them accidentally.

Though Iosua was, physically, very thick-set, with a large head and exceptionally large hands and feet, he was most inconspicuous in class, withdrawn, offering mumbled replies when I asked him questions; he always sat at the back, the true plodder who had studied extra hard to come from the village primary school to Samoa College and who, after two tries at School Certificate, qualified for the sixth form; a solid citizen who would have maintained his inconspicuousness if I hadn't introduced *Hamlet* (the play, that is) to his class.

I've never been one for Shakespeare: my high-school teachers had ruined him for me, and I've always found the language of the plays extremely difficult. But for that fateful year, *Hamlet* was the set play for the University Entrance Exam, and I *had* to teach it. Just imagine: *Hamlet* in the sweltering tropics in a language foreign to students who know little of Europe and castles in Denmark! So I decided I'd just try and teach them enough about the play to get them through the exam. For me also, the always intellectual, perpetually self-questioning Hamlet was a slightly ridiculous, sometimes silly, self-indulgent adolescent constantly

164

picking at his deformed navel, unable to break out of the cerebral. (Mental masturbator! a friend once described him. Masochistic voyeur! was another description.)

Most of the students groaned (not too audibly though) when, one humid sweaty afternoon I announced we were going to study *Hamlet*, starting the next day. I gave out copies of the play and told them to read them. I described the plot briefly, and tried to get them interested by announcing that Laurence Olivier, 'the greatest of all Shakespearean actors', had recorded the play and we would listen to that performance.

The next morning at the start of the period, I put on the first of the long-playing records. The students settled down quickly. I withdrew to the back and, pretending to be following my script and listening to the record, sank into the fuzzy, pleasant world of daydreams. (My usual escape from the boredom of teaching!) The rhythmic flow of the performance, of poetry and sound effects, the attentive silence of the students, became a barely audible tide surging dully at the edge of my hearing. Throughout the years since then, I've kept remembering the faint but annoying smell of fresh cow-shit wafting in from the paddocks only a short distance away. Why has that memory persisted? It's extraneous to this tale. Life is not art, I must remember that. Chaos is more usual than order, the Principle of Uncertainty is built into the cosmos, Pita would say. The smell of fresh cow-shit was there and had nothing to do with *Hamlet*, but it happened! It wasn't an evil omen, the Apparition come to Elsinore Castle! The fact of it was that I was in the belly of a mellow day-dream – probably a lustful one (I was then a very fit, very hedonistic twenty-four-year-old) – while my poor, bored students were trying to cope with the golden Prince who was trying to cope with his golden navel. (Perhaps the mixed-up Prince should've been contemplating his most central organ only a short distance below his navel!) The smell of cow-shit intruded, a coincidence.

I surfaced when the bell rang to end the period. The students started packing their books. One of them turned off the record-player. 'You may leave!' I told the class.

Three boys passed me as I walked up to my desk at the front of the classroom '. . . *Not so, my lord; I am too much in the sun.*' For a moment, I couldn't believe I'd heard it: it was an almost perfect imitation of Olivier, so English and perfect an utterance couldn't have come from any of my students! I recognized Iosua as the middle of the three. No, he would be the last one capable of such mimicry!

Next day I walked into a noisy English class, put on the next record, and the students quietened down at once. As I went to sit at the back, I saw the sentence in red chalk on the back blackboard: 'I AM TOO MUCH IN THE SUN, signed Hamlet'. I didn't say anything about it to the class.

Once, during the next thirty or so minutes of my usual day-dreaming, I noticed the girl next to me nodding to sleep. I coughed. She woke up and smiled. Just beyond her, Iosua was upright with intense attention, his eyes riveted on his script, his lips mouthing the text in time with the actors. At least one of them was excited by the Prince's ordeal, I thought, and then returned to my day-dreaming.

Fifteen minutes before the end of our period the next day, I stopped the record and asked them if they wanted me to explain anything. No requests. (Inwardly, I was relieved because, as yet, I hadn't prepared any detailed explanations.)

'Well, can anyone quote any lines from the play?' (I had to fill in ten minutes, but what a stupid request to make, I thought.) For a short while, there were no offers. Then a thick but timid arm began to rise at the back just under the red sentence, the quotation, on the blackboard. I was reminded of a frightened sunflower, in the morning, unfolding and rising (compelled by its nature) to know the sunlight. 'Yes?' I asked the now upright arm. It was Iosua, eyes still focused on his desk top, the top of his thickly haired head pointing at me. Some girls giggled. 'Yes, Iosua,' I encouraged him.

'I say something from the play?' (Atrocious English!) More giggling. His friends were squirming with him, praying he wasn't going to make a fool of himself.

'Go ahead. You don't have to stand up,' I said. With his head lowered, his face hidden from me, he spoke into his desk-top, almost inaudibly. 'A bit louder,' I said. He raised his head slightly and spoke into the back of the student in front of him. 'Very good!' I said, even though I hadn't heard him clearly. He raised his face towards me at last. Suddenly I remembered a calf being born, breaking out of the slickly wet caul, stretching its limbs, testing them hesitantly, afraid at first, then gaining confidence with each unimpeded stretch.

> '. . . O, that this too too solid flesh would melt.
> Thaw, and resolve itself into a dew.
> Or that the everlasting had not fix'd . . .'

At first it was broken, barely intelligible. A ripple of mirth fluttered through the class.

'That was very good,' I congratulated him, realizing that he had just committed a very courageous act: his peers frowned upon any student who paraded his knowledge or ability in front of a teacher; it wasn't Samoan, it was blatantly papalagi to 'show off' one's individual talents. 'Do you know any more?' I asked. He shook his head.

That evening while I was drinking with friends at the R.S.A. Club, I unexpectedly thought of him and how he had tried so hard to rise above his insignificance, his timidity and fear. For him, the lines had been more than memorized ones, they had been a magical fish-hook fishing him out of the boundaries of himself. I envied his growing courage.

Abruptly the class stopped laughing when I entered the room. I sensed they were trying to hide something from me. I glanced at Iosua. He looked embarrassed. I put on the next record. 'BUT BREAK, MY HEART, FOR I MUST HOLD MY TONGUE signed Hamlet' was scrawled, in bold yellow chalk, across the top of the front blackboard. 'At least one person in this class knows *her* Hamlet!' I joked. Some of them laughed. They all tried not to look at Iosua.

Before the end of the period, I tried it out again. He offered to recite. This time none of us laughed. It was an uncanny and astounding performance. Sitting intensely still in his chair, his eyes slits of concentration, his hands gripping the edge of his desk, he cast the miraculous net of his voice over us, trapping us all.

His accent was still noticeably Samoan, yet it was a spell-binding mimicry of the record. This time, the Ghost:

> *'Ay, that incestuous, that adulterate beast,*
> *With witchcraft of his wits, with traitorous gifts —*
> *O wicked wit and gifts that have the power*
> *So to seduce! — won to his shameful lust*
> *The will of my most virtuous queen . . .'*

As he recited, I thought: what god was speaking through him? What gift was pulling him above his mediocrity? We clapped when he finished. 'Go on, Hamlet!' someone called. He looked at me. I nodded.

> *'. . . Let not the royal bed of Denmark be*
> *A couch of luxury and damned incest.*
> *But howsomever thou pursuest this act,*
> *Taint not thy mind, nor let . . .'*

I sensed then the committed quality of obsession. This wasn't simply a performance: Iosua was discovering his gift for Hamlet, the gift which made him exceptional. How else could you explain his facility to absorb, so easily, uncannily, the record and fury of the Prince's tale?

Some students whistled, we all clapped, he bowed his head once and smiled and was the usual Iosua again, released by the god. 'He knows all of Hamlet's lines!' Mamafa, one of his friends, said. 'Not possible!' a girl challenged. 'Ask him!'

He was soon reciting whole chunks from Hamlet's soliloquies, almost flawlessly. The more he recited, the more confidently he assumed Olivier's voice and delivery. And through his performance and obvious love of Hamlet, I too was, for the first time in my life, falling in love with the play.

That week at the Staff Common Room I asked about him. All his other teachers agreed he wasn't very bright, but worked hard, obeyed his teachers, caused no problems whatsoever, would make a good clerk or civil servant, maybe even a dedicated primary-school teacher. So I kept Iosua's gift to myself.

On Monday morning, I could hear him reciting as I approached the classroom. I entered quietly. He was standing in front of the class. He stopped when he noticed me. I nodded. He continued. I sat down quietly.

He was magnificent. A hypnotic energy emanated from him. He *was* Hamlet, and possessed. Though he did not act, his voice, his presence, performed it all. Such intensity was not of us: it was a terrible beauty.

Later as the class was leaving, I asked him, 'Do you remember other plays as well?' He shook his head. 'Just *Hamlet*?' He nodded. 'Why?'

'I don't know,' he mumbled. 'Hamlet was a great hero.' He was again empty of the god.

Could I have stopped Hamlet from possessing him totally, then? (Or was it the reverse, was he taking possession of Hamlet?) Without Hamlet he would probably have been safe, secure, protected from, unaware of his only gift. (I'm getting carried away again. I'm sure that at that time all I cared about was his miraculous transformation and gift, and about encouraging him to use it. It wasn't until later that I became aware of the danger.)

In our next English lessons, I got other students to read the other roles to his Hamlet.

'Do you understand what you're reciting?' I asked him after the other students had gone.

'A little,' he replied. He looked up at me. In his eyes was a brilliant dazzle: he was high, high on Hamlet.

A day later a science teacher asked me if I was teaching *Hamlet* to the sixth form. That explains it, he laughed when I said yes.

'What?' I asked.

'Our Sixth Form now has a *real* Hamlet. They even get him to perform in my class. He signs all his assignments, Hamlet.'

'I'm sure he's just joking.'

'I hope he is,' he said.

In the Staff Common Room some teachers started joking about our College acquiring 'a very gifted Hamlet who isn't particularly good at anything else'. Fatally flawed! one of them quipped. They laughed. I was annoyed but said nothing.

I began to fear for him.

'Where is Iosua?' I asked at our next English period. Nobody seemed to know. I started the record.

'He has gone home,' Mamafa said. 'He's not well.' I tried to ignore the suppressed wave of laughter which surged through the class.

During that period while *Hamlet* played on, as it were, I couldn't escape my deepening anxiety about Iosua. At the end of the period, Mamafa waited until the other students had left and then told me,

'He is not well. He is afraid.'

'Of what?'

'Of him – Hamlet!'

'But why?'

'He says, Hamlet won't leave him alone.' Mamafa paused and added,

'Miss Monroe, you must help him. The students and teachers are starting to poke fun at him!'

'I'll try,' I promised, though I was heavy with a feeling of helplessness.

'It is as if he is two people. Every time he is Hamlet, which is happening more and more often, he finds it difficult to be himself again . . . What is happening to him?'

'Tell him to come and see me!'

I hardly slept that night, refusing to admit to myself that I had been responsible for Iosua's discovery of his gift, obsession, madness. How was I going to help him? I had to confront that too.

He was away from school for over a week but Mamafa assured me he was well. My anxiety lessened. The day after we finished studying *Hamlet*, the students having completed their notes about the play, and I had told them we were moving into a study of modern poetry, he returned.

While the others were settling down, I asked him if he was all right. He grinned and took his usual seat at the back.

And for a couple of weeks, while we struggled through some modern poetry, he was again his usual withdrawn self, empty of the gift, offering little to our understanding of the poetry and understanding little of it. He even massacred a poem I got him to read aloud to the class. Further proof, to me, of his dull normality. I was elated he was safe, but I sensed in the class a feeling of disappointment that Hamlet had left us and we were again mired in our uninspired, boring normality without vision or daring, trapped in our perpetually deadening sanity. Better a plodding, normal Iosua though than an insane Hamlet, I persuaded myself! (I wasn't going to be responsible for a kid going crackers!)

Once again we forgot him in his inconspicuousness.

171

'WITHOUT HIM I AM NOBODY' in red chalk on the front blackboard when I walked into my classroom before school started. Momentarily I was puzzled. A Jesus freak, I concluded. Lines from a hymn. I rubbed it off, sat down at my desk, and started working.

Next morning the same lines appeared in exactly the same place. A very persistent Jesus freak! Again, I erased it.

'WITHOUT

WITHOUT THE

WITHOUT THE PRINCE

WITHOUT THE PRINCE I

WITHOUT THE PRINCE I AM

WITHOUT THE PRINCE I AM NOBODY'

Good poem, I thought when I saw it, the following morning. I erased it, and before I left school that day wrote in the same place:

'YOU ARE NOT NOBODY

YOU ARE A POET

AND DON'T KNOW IT'

I went straight to my classroom the next morning.

'MISS MONROE

LOVES THE PRINCE

BUT THE PRINCE WENT MAD'

Annoyed. Puzzled. My anxiety jabbing at me again, I found myself rubbing that off quickly, unwilling and afraid to explore the extraordinary.

'Have any of you poets in this class been writing their brilliant verse on my blackboard?' I asked my sixth form that afternoon. They all looked puzzled.

The next morning – and I still remember the persistent light rain sweeping across the classroom windows – I immediately identified, with erupting fear, my mysterious poet when I read this on the blackboard:

'TO

TO BE

TO BE OR

TO BE OR NOT

TO BE OR NOT TO

TO BE OR NOT TO BE'

I didn't see him that day because I didn't have his class. My fear, tinged with guilt, became disturbingly persistent. At the same time, I began to experience an irrepressible curiosity to penetrate more into that terrible beauty and discover where he was at. Was he still possessed? Beyond the ordinary, touched by the gods? So before going home that day I wrote:

'THAT

THAT IS

THAT IS THE

THAT IS THE QUESTION'

His reply was simple (and really put the shits up me!).

'THE CHOICE IS NOT TO BE'

I kept imagining him using all sorts of violent methods to commit suicide, as I waited for his class to appear. My other classes passed in a frantic daze and I made frequent trips to the toilet to relieve my fear. I could've hugged him to death when he came as his usual normal self and grinned at me as he sat down. During the lesson I persuaded myself that my fears were unfounded.

I stayed after school in my small office to do some marking, and forgot about him quickly as I attacked the stack of assignments. 4.00 p.m. I shut the last exercise book and discovered I was uncomfortably sticky with sweat, and thought of a long cold shower. I looked out into the classroom. He was at the blackboard writing. His huge arm danced across its surface, leaving these words behind:

'MISS MONROE

THE PRINCE IS NOT

TO BE'

With intense fascination I observed him, knowing he was unaware of my presence.

Turning dramatically to face his audience of empty desks, he began his performance. The light from the upper louvres was like gold on his face; his eyes blazed with a holy fire, his rhythm and movement were flowing and sure and poetic, as he was transformed into Hamlet contemplating the beauty of the abyss, fascinated by it, vulnerable to it, tempting it. I tried not to watch but even my guilt tasted brilliantly sweet as I witnessed that magnificent hero making love to his self-indulgent fascination with madness and death, risking all. Strangely, yet not strangely, I discovered that my voyeurism was becoming unashamedly sexual as he courted death unconditionally.

> . . . *To die, to sleep –*
> *No more; and by a sleep to say we end*
> *The heartache and the thousand natural shocks*
> *That flesh is heir to. 'Tis a consummation*
> *Devoutly to be wished.*
> *To die, to sleep;*
> *To sleep, perchance to dream . . .'*

Suddenly I wanted him to see me and stop (and thus stop me from enjoying his tragic dance), but he continued to advance over the abyss, fingering his own contemplation of his death, picking at it, tempting himself, dancing step by step closer to the eye of the abyss.

I moved forward. Too late. Still unaware of me, he swung towards the front door and, still caught in Hamlet's voice, swept out. *Exit.*

Through my tears, I watched him stride, his head held high, his whole body in command of the world, across the lushly green school grounds descending to the main road. Away, diminishing in size with each brave step, with the palms, flame trees and the sky applauding. Hamlet, Prince. Conqueror of the Abyss!

He didn't return to school ever.

Mamafa told me that Iosua had been sent by his parents to live with relatives in New Zealand and attend school there. That salved my conscience; I didn't even check the truth of Mamafa's information – I didn't want to face the possibility that Iosua was insane and in a hospital! I wanted to live with a sane Iosua, a diligent student, in a prosperous New Zealand!

Good art would have me leave him, in my tale, suspended in a suspenseful bout of heroic madness, with the awed reader applauding his courage, but, alas, life is more tragic (and dreadful) than that.

Six or so years later when I was holidaying in New Zealand, I visited relatives in Porirua and was waiting at the crowded station for a train into Wellington, when someone tapped me lightly on the shoulder. I ignored it, thinking it was someone trying to pick me up. A more insistent tap. I turned sharply and cringed immediately. He was huge, a bulging-all-over Michelin Man with that unmistakable grin and a little girl sleeping in his arms. He nodded. Automatically I shook his hand and kissed him on the cheek.

'It is you, isn't it?' he asked hesitantly in Samoan.

'Yes. Are you well?' I replied in Samoan.

Nodding his head, he said, 'Yes, I am well. And you, Miss Monroe?' He was my student again, even the voice, the respect.

'I am well, thank you. Is that your daughter?' I caressed the girl's back.

'Yes. I have two other children.' In his awkward, almost inarticulate way he told me he was a foreman in a factory which manufactured mattresses, and lived with his wife, children and five other relatives, in a low-rent state house. Then wistfully, as if it was too painful to say it, he admitted, 'I had a bit of illness.'

'Yes, I remember,' I joked.

His eyes lit up. 'It didn't last long,' he chuckled. 'I've been well ever since.'

'That's good,' I heard myself say, with the heroic image of him marching over the school fields caught in the heart of my head. Hamlet, I yearned to say to him. The magic word could free him once again.

'Are you still teaching?'

'No.' I was suddenly lost for anything else to say. The train was pulling into the platform and passengers were surging towards it.

'Would you like to visit our home?' he invited me.

'Thank you, but I have to go back into Wellington. I'm returning to Samoa tomorrow.' The lie was automatic, final, I didn't want to see what had become of Hamlet in the suburbs. I bent forward and kissed his daughter on the cheek. 'Goodbye!'

'Here,' he said, sheathing money in my coat pocket. 'Please!' he pleaded when I tried to return it to him.

'Goodbye!' I started hurrying to the open door of the carriage.

'Goodbye. May you have a safe journey!' he called.

The train started moving. I looked back and waved. In the milling crowd, his size, his shape, his aloneness made him look so apart, distinct. He waved slowly as if he was waving a heavy flag. I recalled how, in my class, he had first raised his timid arm and had volunteered to quote from *Hamlet*. I struggled to push the memory out of my heart but couldn't.

I wept silently.

> *Iosua*
> *Hamlet*
> *Prince for a dazzling day*
> *But better that one passionate day*
> *than never at all*